Her love ce
wiped aw ss
and longi

But the mouth which sought her own rested only briefly on her yielding lips.

'Forgive me!' Giles said hoarsely. 'I have no right to touch you...no right at all.'

Gina stared at him. She could not have been more shocked if he had struck her.

'Who has a better right?' she asked in amazement. 'Were we not promised to each other? We swore that we would never change...do you remember?'

'I do. Perhaps we have not changed, but our circumstances are different now...' Giles turned and took a few paces away from her. 'I have nothing to offer you, Gina...'

'Have I ever asked for anything? All I ever wanted was your love. I thought you felt the same.'

A young woman disappears.
A husband is suspected of murder.
Stirring times for all the neighbourhood in

Book 13

When the debauched Marquis of Sywell won
Steepwood Abbey years ago at cards, it led to the death
of the then Earl of Yardley. Now he's caused scandal
again by marrying a girl out of his class—and young
enough to be his granddaughter! After being married
only a short time, the Marchioness has disappeared,
leaving no trace of her whereabouts. There is every
expectation that yet more scandals will emerge, though
no one yet knows just how shocking they will be.

The four villages surrounding the Steepwood Abbey
estate are in turmoil, not only with the dire goings-on
at the Abbey, but also with their own affairs. Each
story in **The Steepwood Scandal** follows the mystery
behind the disappearance of the young woman, and the
individual romances of lovers connected in some way
with the intrigue.

Regency Drama
intrigue, mischief...and marriage

MR RUSHFORD'S HONOUR

Meg Alexander

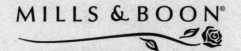

MILLS & BOON®

*First published in Great Britain 2002
Harlequin Mills & Boon Limited,
Eton House, 18-24 Paradise Road, Richmond, Surrey TW9 1SR*

© Harlequin Books S.A. 2002

Special thanks and acknowledgement are given to Meg Alexander for her contribution to The Steepwood Scandal series.

ISBN 0 263 82854 9

*Set in Times Roman 10½ on 12½ pt.
119-0502-57285*

*Printed and bound in Spain
by Litografia Rosés S.A., Barcelona*

After living in southern Spain for many years, **Meg Alexander** now lives in Kent, although, having been born in Lancashire, she feels that her roots are in the north of England. Meg's career has encompassed a wide variety of roles, from professional cook to assistant director of a conference centre. She has always been a voracious reader, and loves to write. Other loves include history, cats, gardening, cooking and travel. She has a son and two grandchildren.

Mr Rushford's Honour features characters you will have already met in *The Reluctant Bride*, Meg Alexander's previous novel in **The Steepwood Scandal**.

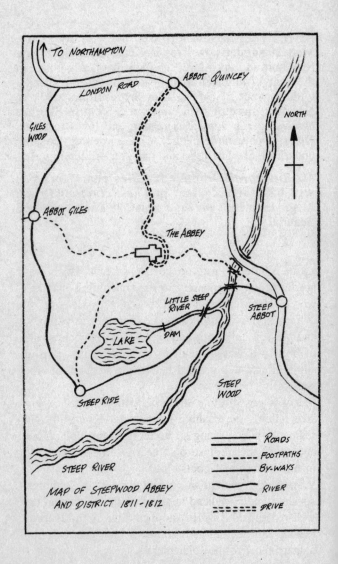

MAP OF STEEPWOOD ABBEY
AND DISTRICT 1811 - 1812

Chapter One

Spring 1812

Gina Whitelaw was no beauty—a fact which was not immediately apparent to the watching bystanders who clustered about her coach.

Too short by a full head to be described as willowy, and blessed only with hair of an indeterminate shade of brown, it was difficult to understand the gasp of admiration which greeted her as she stepped into the street.

It was possibly the sheer perfection of her expensive toilette, the dashing bonnet, the beautifully cut redingote which clung so lovingly to her voluptuous curves, or the glimpse of a neatly turned ankle clad in fine leather half-boots.

A passing gentleman noticed none of these things. As she turned her head to speak to her coachman the well-remembered voice stopped him in mid-stride, leaving him feeling as if someone had just dealt him a sharp blow to the solar plexus.

Gina had not seen him. He stepped into the doorway across the street, feasting his eyes upon the face
which had haunted him for the past ten years.

She hadn't changed much in all that time. He
would have known her anywhere. The brilliant blue
gaze was just the same, as was the enchanting smile
which curved that generous mouth.

His feelings threatened to overwhelm him. Surely
she must sense his closeness. The bond between them
had been so strong. Had they not agreed together that
they were two halves of one whole? He waited, will-
ing her to reach out to him across the years, but the
separation had been too long. The old magic which
had made them aware of the presence of each other
at a distance had clearly vanished.

She turned away and walked into the house, smiling and chatting to the two girls who accompanied
her.

Giles shuddered. Could they be her own? A moment's reflection convinced him that it was impossible. The girls were well-grown teenagers. He looked
again at the coach, and recognised the Whitelaw crest
emblazoned on the doors. Clearly Gina was still
connected with the family, but in what capacity? He
was no expert in the finer points of fashion, but the
exquisitely dressed creature who stepped down just a
moment ago was obviously not a servant. Had
Whitelaw made her his mistress? He clenched his
fists until the knuckles whitened, miserably aware that
he was fully deserving of the agony the notion
caused him.

He had left her without a word of explanation, in a foreign country, and at the beck and call of her employers. He could only blame himself if Gina had taken the route followed by many another.

He was only half aware of the buzz of speculation which surrounded him. With the excitement of the new arrival over, the crowd was drifting away. Snatches of their conversation reached his ears.

''Tis high time the old Mansion House was taken,' an elderly woman assured her friend. ''Twill be good for trade to have some new blood in the village.'

'Aye! There will be many as will hope to make their fortune on the back of that young creature's spending.'

'I make no doubt she can afford it,' the first speaker said. 'The place is bought, not rented, so I hear, and at a price that you would not believe.' She named a figure which made her companion gasp. 'The builders are in already,' she continued.

'But who is she? And why come to Abbot Quincey? She looks to me more like a townie than a countrywoman. Them with money prefers the life in Lunnon, especially at her age.'

'Don't you know her? Oh I forgot, you being an in-comer an' all. She'd gone by the time you came to live here. I recognised her at once. 'Tis Gina Westcott, the baker's daughter.'

'Oh my! I thought she was a lady.' The note of disappointment in the second speaker's voice was clear. 'Ain't she the one who ran away to see the world?'

'Some such nonsense!' her friend agreed. 'Looks to me as if she's seen more than the world...' A leer accompanied this remark and brought a chuckle from the other woman.

Giles flushed with anger and moved away before he was tempted into a sharp retort. He turned into the Angel, and early as it was, he ordered a glass of brandy. Then he strolled over to the window and gazed back down the street towards the Mansion House.

What on earth had persuaded Gina to come back to Abbot Quincey? The snide remarks that he had overheard would be the first of many. She would be exposed to every kind of rumour and speculation. No one would call upon her, and she faced a life of bitter loneliness.

He could do nothing for her. Had it not been for his sister's splendid marriage he would be living upon his uncle's charity and the kind invitations of his friends. Sipping his drink, he sighed as he reflected upon the past ten years. Summoned from Italy and Gina's arms, he had returned to Abbot Quincey at his uncle's request in an attempt to save the family fortunes.

It had all been in vain. Hard as he had worked to restore the estate so badly neglected by his charming but feckless father, all had been lost on that dreadful night last year when Gareth Rushford had gambled away the last of his patrimony. Worse had followed when the father whom they loved in spite of his weakness had been crushed to death in a carriage accident.

'Cheer up, old fellow! It can't be as bad as all that!'

Giles turned to find his brother-in-law beside him.

Giles smiled in spite of himself. After an uneasy start he had grown fond of his eldest sister's husband.

'Will you join me, Isham?' He gestured towards his glass.

'I think I'd better if you are about to crush me with some dire news.' Isham signalled to the landlord. 'What is it, Giles? You look as though you've seen a ghost.'

'In a way I have. It is just that…well…I caught a glimpse of someone I used to know.'

'I hope he isn't about to run you through. What have you been up to?'

'It's nothing like that. And it isn't a "he". It's a "she".'

'Oh dear! As bad as that?' Isham began to smile. 'Speak to the lady, Giles. I'm sure she will forgive you…'

'I fear she won't. It is too late for that.' For a minute Giles was tempted to confide in the tall figure beside him. Then he thought better of it. There was Gina's good name to consider. He made an effort to change the subject. 'What are you doing here?' he asked.

'I'm planning to call upon an old friend. The promise was made some time ago.'

'And India isn't with you? She isn't ill, I hope?'

'On the contrary. She is in the best of health, if a little queasy in the mornings… She has been awaiting your return from Bristol for these past ten days or more.'

'We were much delayed.' Giles gave his brother-in-law a rueful smile. 'Mama determined upon a triumphal progress to receive the congratulations of her friends upon Letty's betrothal. I thought we'd never see Abbot Quincey again.' He hesitated. 'Anthony, I didn't mean to stay away so long. I feel I've let you down...about managing the estate, I mean.'

'Nonsense. If you had to be away it was best to go before the spring, and the ladies could not have travelled without an escort. In any case, I was glad you were not here when Henry died.'

Giles gripped his hand in quick sympathy. 'What a brute I am not to have offered you my condolences! That was a bad business. How is his mother now?'

'Lucia is recovering slowly...' Lord Isham gazed into space. Best to let Giles believe that the man the world had regarded as his half-brother had died defending his loved ones from the mob. Only India and Henry's mother knew the truth of it beside himself. Henry, not knowing that he was no blood relative to Isham, had come to the Grange that dreadful night to remove both India and his lordship from his path, believing that he would inherit title, wealth and lands. The mob he led would be used to cloak the murders. By a strange twist of fate he had been killed himself by a single shot fired by one of the Luddites.

'Have the authorities caught the man?' Giles was forced to repeat his question twice.

'What?' Recalled to the present, Isham shook his

head. 'I doubt if they ever will. The crowd was huge and it was dark. Now we are met by a wall of silence.' He glanced at his watch. 'Forgive me, Giles, but I am late. I must present myself at the Mansion House without delay.'

He had not expected his words to produce the effect they did. Giles stiffened and went pale.

'The Mansion House? Why, who…I mean…do you know the people there?'

'Lady Whitelaw has just bought the place. Her husband was one of my closest friends.'

'Great heavens, is her ladyship still alive? When I knew her she was at death's door.'

'When was that?' Isham was clearly puzzled.

'It was ten years ago…in Italy.' Giles forced out the words through stiff lips. 'She was not expected to live beyond the year's end.'

Isham's brow cleared. 'Oh, you are thinking of Whitelaw's first wife. Gina is blooming, as you may see for yourself if you accompany me. She married Whitelaw two years later. Did you not meet her when you were in Italy?'

'Yes…! No…!' Giles was reeling under a second shock that morning. Suddenly, he felt that his high cravat was choking him. If he didn't get away he would betray himself. His little Gina married to a man almost old enough to be her grandfather! It didn't bear thinking of. He made his excuses quickly.

'Another time, perhaps? I must go. Mother and Letty will be waiting. We'll see you at the Grange.'

'I shan't be long. The call is merely to see if Gina

needs help in settling in.' Isham accompanied him into the street and turned in the direction of the Mansion House.

Giles felt more confused than ever. If Gina had a husband why would she need Isham's help? He was burning to know the answer and cursed himself for a coward, knowing in his heart that he had been unable to face her. What must she think of him, if, indeed, she thought of him at all?

He wasn't proud of his behaviour. She had been such an open, friendly child, sixteen at the most. And at twenty how was he himself to know that what had started as a teasing, laughing friendship would develop so quickly into a passionate love affair.

His thoughts grew sombre. They had been so young, the pair of them. Perhaps, for her, the pain of that sudden separation had not struck so deep. There would have been bewilderment, a few tears, and possibly anger. Then she would have forgotten him. As he had forgotten her?

His lips twisted in a bitter grimace. Not a day had passed when she was absent from his thoughts.

On his return to England he had written to her, but she had not replied. In a Europe plunged once more into the turmoil of war after the collapse of the Treaty of Amiens he could not be sure that she had ever received his letters, or indeed, if she and the Whitelaw family were still alive. He had no way of finding them. All his enquiries had been fruitless, and Napoleon's armies still ravaged the continent of Europe.

How many nights had he lain awake picturing unknown horrors? Sometimes he'd imagined her lifeless corpse beneath a pile of shattered masonry. He'd tried to close his eyes to a more terrifying fate. Gina might have been taken alive by an advancing army. He was under no illusion as to what would have happened then.

Now he made an effort to recover his composure. His worst fears had not been realised. Clearly, Gina was well and happy. For that, at least, he must be thankful, though he must face the fact that she was finally lost to him.

Something of the strain he was feeling must have shown upon his face. His sister noticed it at once.

'Giles, is anything amiss?' she asked quietly.

'You may well ask, Letty!' Mrs Rushford's look of anxiety gave way to an expression of annoyance. 'My dear boy, where have you been? I was persuaded that you had met with an accident. We have been waiting for you this age. I must hope that I haven't caught a chill, standing about in this sharp wind.'

'Mother, you should have waited in the coach.'

'We have not been here above a minute,' Letty assured him. 'Hammonds had the goods we needed. It took some time to choose.'

Mrs Rushford tossed her head, 'That's as maybe! It does not take long for a woman of my delicate state of health to fall victim to an affliction of the lungs.'

'I'm sorry to have kept you waiting. I met Isham in the town.'

'Was India with him?' Mrs Rushford's petulant expression didn't change. 'Do you tell me that they knew that we were here, and didn't come to greet us?'

'Isham was alone.' Giles handed the ladies into the coach. 'India is waiting at the Grange. She didn't expect us until later in the day.'

'Did I not say that there was no necessity to leave at such a ridiculously early hour this morning? But you would have it, Giles. All this rushing about will do my health no good at all. Had it not been for the invitation from Lady Wells I should not have considered travelling in the winter.'

Letty squeezed her mother's hand. 'But now it is the spring. Besides, you did it for me, and you dealt with Lady Wells so beautifully. In the end she raised no objection to my engagement to Oliver.'

'I should think not indeed. She may consider herself fortunate to have formed a connection with the Ishams. It was far more than she might have hoped for in the marriage of a younger son. The woman is a positive toad-eater! I gave her a sharp set-down or two. Such pretensions! Isham will put her in her place, I make no doubt.'

Letty made haste to change the subject of her fearsome mother-in-law to be.

'How is India? I have missed her so.'

'Why Letty, she is blooming, so I hear, though Isham mentioned that she had been queasy...'

To his astonishment this innocuous piece of information resulted in his gaining his mother's full attention.

'Queasy, you say? Thank heavens for that! Oh,

where is Isham? I must talk to him at once.' Mrs Rushford leaned out of the carriage window and began to scan the street.

'Mother, don't distress yourself. India is not seriously ill.'

'Of course she isn't, you foolish creature! She is probably with child. Oh, drat the man! He is large enough for anyone to see him. Where can he have got to?'

'He is paying a call on Lady Whitelaw,' Giles said stiffly.

'Lady Whitelaw? Who is she? I have not heard the name before…'

'She has taken the old Mansion House…bought it, I believe…'

Mrs Rushford settled back against the leather cushions, her good humour quite restored. 'Splendid! Splendid! I shall call upon her without delay. Does Isham know her well?'

'Her husband is a friend of his.' Giles signalled to the coachman and the carriage rolled away. This was not the time to explain that Lady Whitelaw was the former Gina Westcott, the baker's daughter. Even her title might not be enough to wipe away that taint of trade.

Then he smiled to himself. Isham was more than a match for his snobbish mother-in-law. If he decreed that Lady Whitelaw was a welcome visitor, both she and her husband would be invited to the Grange.

For his own part, the thought filled him with trepidation. How was he to face her? Had his circumstances been different he would have gone away at once, but now, as estate manager, he was tied to the place.

She herself might refuse the invitation when she realised that Isham was married to his sister. On the other hand, she might accept, longing for revenge, and prepared to rejoice in his discomfiture. He lapsed into silence. He would have given much to have heard the result of Isham's interview with Gina.

It would not have comforted him. Gina had welcomed her visitor with every appearance of pleasure.

Apparently untroubled by the bustle about her, she hurried towards his lordship holding out both her hands.

'Anthony, you are a genius! How did you find this place?'

'It wasn't difficult,' he teased. 'No one had moved it.' Isham glanced about him. 'Will it suit you, Gina?'

'It is perfect…exactly what I wanted!' The vivid little face was alive with enthusiasm. 'It was good of you to attend to all the details for me. I could never have done it from Scotland. My dear, I hated to ask you when you had so much else to think about.'

'You didn't ask me…I offered,' he said lightly. 'I'm always at your service. You must remember that.'

'How can I forget it? You have done so much for me and the girls.' She laid a sympathetic hand upon his arm. 'I was so sorry to hear of your brother's death.'

'As was I to hear of the death of Whitelaw. He was always a good friend to me.'

'He was one of the kindest people I ever met,' she said simply. 'I was lucky to have known him.'

'He felt the same, my dear. He never tired of singing your praises. I can't think what the family would have done without you. How are the girls?'

'They are growing fast. I have two young ladies on my hands. Mair will have her Season next year.'

'Great heavens! It doesn't seem possible. I thought that they were still children.'

'They are, in a way, but the young grow up before one knows it.' Gina smiled. 'Enough about our concerns…will you bring your wife to see me soon? We were all so delighted to learn of your marriage.'

The harsh face of her companion softened into an expression of the utmost tenderness. 'I love her dearly, Gina, and now, though it is early days, we may have a child before the year is out.'

He made no attempt to disguise his delight and Gina jumped up and kissed him.

'That is the best news in the world! Now you shall not bring her into Abbot Quincey over these dreadful roads. I shall come to you when it is convenient.' Gina paused. 'Does she know who I am?'

'I haven't discussed your affairs with anyone, but what difference can it make?'

She gave him a speculative look. 'Never forget that I was the daughter of the baker in this village, Anthony. That fact will not sit well with everyone.'

She saw his face darken and made haste to reassure

him. 'You must not be angry with me. You, of all people, would not marry a petty-minded woman, but there are others who will not take so generous a view.'

'Shall you care? I had thought that with this house and your title and…er…'

'The fortune? Well, I won't be mealy-mouthed about it. All that will help, but my antecedents will not be forgotten. I would not put your wife in a difficult position…'

Isham laughed aloud. 'You do not know her yet. If there is one person likely to champion your cause it will be India. She tells me that I am a law unto myself, but the same applies to her.'

'Even so, I feel that you should tell her about my former life. I did run away from here, you know.'

'At fifteen, wasn't it? I've often wondered about that. What made you leave your family? You took a dreadful chance, you know.'

'I wanted to see the world.' Gina was absorbed in straightening the fringe upon her cuff and she didn't look at him. 'I went in search of adventure.' It wasn't the whole truth, but it was as much as she would admit to.

'Well, you certainly found that.' Isham looked at the bent head and wondered. 'Whitelaw told me often of your courage in facing bandits and mutinous seamen. Doesn't anything frighten you?'

'There was no point in being frightened.' She gave him a merry look. 'Much better to learn to use a pistol well and be prepared to use it. It is a powerful persuader in places such as India, especially when one does not speak the language.'

'A telling argument, if ever I heard one!' Isham laughed again. 'Did you find the same in Europe and the Caribbean?'

'I did.' She shared in his amusement and then the laughter faded from her eyes. 'There were the girls to think about,' she said quietly. 'And her ladyship grew worse throughout our travels, though Whitelaw searched unceasingly for a cure. When she died I thought that he would not recover.'

'You were devoted to both of them, I think.'

'I owed them so much. Oh, Anthony, even at fifteen I was not a complete fool. Had I not gone to them as nursemaid to the girls I might have lived a very different life, that is, if I had survived.'

Isham rose to his feet. 'You are a born survivor, Gina. I have no doubt of that. After a brush with bandits a few old tabbies won't distress you with their gossip. Now you will let me know if there is aught that I can do for you?'

'I will.' Gina held out her hand. 'Thank you again, my friend. I'm sure we will be happy here.'

But Isham was still wondering as he walked back to the smithy. Why had Gina returned to Abbot Quincey when she might have settled anywhere in the country?

There was some hidden agenda, he was sure of it, sensing a certain reserve in the normally open manner of his old friend's wife. It wasn't like her, and it troubled him.

Had she returned to her birthplace with the intention of paying off old scores? No, that would be totally out of character. He would not even suspect her of a very human wish to flaunt her good fortune in front of those who might previously have despised her. That was not Gina. He knew her to be cheerful, dependable, and painfully honest. But there was something. He shook his head and went to find his horse.

Meantime, Gina was lost in thought. Her plans were going well, but there was still much to do. She looked up smiling as Mair and Elspeth came to find her.

'Do you like your rooms?' she asked.

Mair settled down beside her, resting her head against Gina's knee. 'Perfection!' she said in a dreamy tone. 'You were so clever to find this place.'

'We have Lord Isham to thank for that,' she told them. 'You have just missed him.'

'Oh, no!' Elspeth was dismayed. Her hero-worship of his lordship had been the cause of much teasing within the family. 'When is he to call again?'

'We are to call upon Lord Isham and his wife,' Gina said firmly. 'Now Elspeth, do not pull a face. It is unbecoming. We are to wish his lordship happy, as you must agree.'

'I thought he would not marry,' Elspeth said ungraciously. 'At least until...'

'Until you were old enough to wed him?' Mair giggled. 'By that time he'd be in his dotage...'

'Really, girls, this will not do! I will not have you

speak so of a family friend. Now we have much to do. How does cook go on? I told her that our nuncheon should be light today. We shall eat it now. Then you may get back to your books.'

There was a united cry of despair.

'Must we?' Mair pleaded.

'Indeed you must. Have I not explained so often the importance of an education?'

'But darling Gina, there is so much time for that.' Mair held her stepmother's hand against her cheek. 'May we not have a holiday, just for this one day?'

Gina glanced down at the fiery head. 'Sometimes I despair of you,' she scolded. 'It has taken me a full ten years to educate myself. Now the task is in your own hands, if you will but take advantage of it.'

Elspeth took her other hand. 'But you will help us, Gina, won't you? Suppose we promise to work twice as hard tomorrow? You can't mean to keep our noses to the grindstone all the time.'

'I haven't seen much evidence of that,' Gina said solemnly. Then Mair looked up at her and saw the laughter in her eyes.

'Why, Elspeth, she doesn't mean a word of it.' She jumped up, drawing Gina to her feet and grasping her sister's other hand. 'Time for a war-dance!' she announced.

Whooping and stamping, the two girls drew their stepmother into a ring, chanting as they moved around.

'Now we live in Abbot Quincey
All our parties will be princely.'

Gina shuddered. 'That is certainly the worst verse I have ever heard. And which parties are these?'

The girls whirled her even faster.

'Why, those that we give at my come-out,' Mair cried breathlessly. 'Shall we astonish the village, Gina?'

'Nothing is more certain if you go on like this. I doubt if you will have to wait till then. The servants will be persuaded that we have run mad…'

This did not appear to be the case. The butler apparently found nothing untoward in the sight of his young mistress cavorting about the salon with her stepdaughters. Had he not been mindful of the need for a wooden expression he might have permitted himself a smile. As it was he announced that nuncheon was served, remarking only to the housekeeper that Madam seemed to be in the best of spirits.

'And high time too. Madam is allus cheerful, but what a life she's had! Naught but caring for the sick, as far as I can tell.' Mrs Long gave him a speculative look. 'Think you that she'll settle here?'

'Who can tell?' Hanson had long ceased to wonder at the vagaries of his employers. 'Shall you prefer it, Mrs Long?'

'I don't know yet, but there must be more life here than in the wilds of Scotland. Madam will be thinking of finding husbands for the girls within a year or two, and we ain't so far from London.'

'True! I expect that she will open up the London house this year. I'd welcome it, you know. The place was like a morgue when last I saw it.'

'Her ladyship will change all that. Why, she might even find a husband of her own.'

Hanson bent his head in grave agreement. 'The family is out of mourning now. We may expect visits from every fortune-hunter in the country.'

'Then I hope that you will see them off, Mr Hanson.'

'I shall certainly do my best.' With that promise the butler left his confidante and proceeded to his duties.

Finding a husband was far from Gina's mind as she rose from the dining-table.

'Girls, I have a private call to make this afternoon. I shall not be away for long. Will you occupy yourselves?'

'We shall explore the cellars and the attics,' Elspeth promised. 'This house is a perfect maze of secret places.'

Gina nodded. Then she hurried away to change her fashionable walking dress for a plain toilette. She waved aside Hanson's suggestion of the carriage and turned left along the High Street, gazing at the old familiar surroundings with a pang of nostalgia. Abbot Quincey had not changed since her departure all those years ago and she recognised several of the passers-by, but her bonnet hid her face and no one greeted her.

A ten-minute walk brought her to her destination. The old sign was still above the shop and the door was open, but she hesitated by the window. She had rehearsed this moment for so long, but now her courage threatened to desert her.

Her heart was pounding painfully, but she took a few deep breaths. Then she walked into the shop.

'Yes, Madam? May I help you?' The woman behind the counter was an older, plumper version of Gina herself.

'Don't you know me, Mother?' Gina was close to tears.

'Gina?' Eliza Westcott paled as she peered into her daughter's face. 'Is it really you? Oh, my love, I thought that you were lost to us for ever.' She threw out her arms and Gina hurried to her.

'There, don't cry, Mama. I am home again.'

'You wicked, wicked girl!' Mrs Westcott was raining kisses upon her daughter's face. 'I can't think why you left us in the first place. The worry almost killed us.'

'That was foolish, Mama. I wrote to you each month.'

'But from all those outlandish places, Gina. I had never heard of one half of them. You might have been murdered in your bed.'

'But I wasn't. And you knew I was safe in Scotland for these past few years.'

Mrs Westcott sniffed. 'Safe in Scotland, indeed! There's another wild place, or so I hear.'

'The natives are quite friendly.' Gina began to smile. 'Is Father better now?' She had gleaned little from her mother's infrequent letters.

'He is quite stout again, but still so cross with you.' Mrs Westcott paused. 'When you went away he blamed himself, you see. He still feels that he did not do his duty by you.'

'That isn't true, and I shall tell him so. Where is Father now?'

'He's in the bakery. Come through, my love, and sit by the fire. I will fetch him for you.'

Gina waited in some trepidation. As the youngest of the Westcott children she had been the apple of her father's eye. She could understand his hurt, and she did not expect immediate forgiveness.

When she looked at the cold face she knew that she was right. He would not look her fully in the eye.

'Come to honour us with a visit, your ladyship?' he sneered. 'I thank you for your condescension.'

'I came because I am now free to do so, Father. As you know, my husband died last year. It has taken me some time to settle his affairs.'

'So now you are come to queen it in the village? Well, good luck to you! You won't be needing the likes of us.'

'I've always needed you,' Gina said quietly. 'I'm sorry if I caused you hurt.' She went to him and took his hand. 'Won't you forgive me, Father dear?' She kissed his hand and raised it to her cheek.

It was too much for the master baker. With a groan he took his daughter in his arms and muffled his face against her hair. 'You bad girl! What are we to do with you?' His cheeks were wet and Gina hugged him close.

He took some time to recover his composure, but at last he smiled at her.

'Well, Missy, when are you off again on your adventures?'

'Never, I hope! I've taken the Mansion House in the village… The girls are with me, of course.'

George Westcott whistled in amazement. 'You are flying high, my girl. That must have cost you a pretty penny.'

'Whitelaw left me well provided for, Father. Tell me, how are William and Julia?'

'Both well, I'm glad to say.' Westcott's face softened. 'Wait until you see your nieces and nephews. Your brother's little lads are as merry as grigs, and as to the young maids…'

'Don't get him started on the subject, Gina. To hear your father talk you would think that better girls had never been born. If the truth be told they twist him round their little fingers.' Mrs Westcott looked wistful. 'I could wish that you had children of your own, my dear. When you married we hoped… Well, perhaps it was not to be.'

Gina did not reply. This was no time to explain that her marriage had been one of convenience. Dearly as he loved her, Lord Whitelaw had made that clear. Never strong and no longer young, he was well aware that in the natural order of things he would die before her. Caring for her stepdaughters would be a grave responsibility. He had no wish to add to her burdens by leaving her with children of her own.

Gina had understood and she respected his decision, though she'd known it was not the full truth. For Alistair Whitelaw no woman would ever take the place of his beloved first wife. Her own marriage had been based upon trust and affection. She had never resented it, though her own heart had been given long ago.

She thrust aside the painful memories and picked up her bonnet. 'You will come to see me, won't you?'

Mrs Westcott looked at her husband. Then she nodded. 'We'll come in a day or two. Your Uncle Samuel and Aunt Mary are to visit us tomorrow with the children. You won't want a houseful.'

Gina's polite enquiry as to the welfare of her relatives was less than enthusiastic, but her parents noticed nothing amiss. For her own part her father's brother was the last person she wished to see. Now a wealthy grain merchant, she could only be thankful that he was based in London. At some time in the future she would be forced to meet him again. As yet she was not ready to do so.

For the moment another unavoidable meeting filled her mind. Had she made the right decision in coming back to Abbot Quincey? For all she knew Giles might be married and a father. She had not dared to ask about him, fearing she would give herself away. Well, she would cross her bridges when she came to them.

She kissed her parents and walked back to the Mansion House.

Chapter Two

Had she but known it, Giles was at that moment being forced to listen to a long discussion about the latest resident of Abbot Quincey.

Having satisfied herself that her elder daughter was indeed with child, Mrs Rushford proceeded to acquaint herself with all the latest gossip.

'So much has happened since we went to Bristol,' she announced. 'Now, India, you must tell me everything. Who is this Lady Whitelaw? Giles said that Isham went to call on her this morning… She and her husband will be such an asset to the village.'

'Not her husband, Mama. Lady Whitelaw is a widow…'

Giles had stiffened, but his mother did not notice. 'Well, I expect that she will soon make friends. Is she elderly?'

'She must be twenty-six at most.' India smiled.

'And she has taken the Mansion House? She must be well-to-do…' Mrs Rushford gave her son a look of speculation. The widow, though not young, was not yet at her last prayers, and Giles was in need of a wife. If she brought a handsome dowry with her so much the better. 'When are we to meet her?' she enquired.

'Anthony will let us know. I expect that she has much to do, as she only arrived this morning. He promised to give her an open invitation.'

'Then he knows her well?'

'He was a close friend of her husband.' India hesitated. 'You know her yourself, Mama.'

'How can that be? To my knowledge I have never met the Whitelaws.'

'You have met Lady Whitelaw. She was the former Gina Westcott…'

'The baker's daughter?' Mrs Rushford gave a cry of indignation. 'India, you can't be serious! How can you receive a person who was engaged in trade? What of your social position?'

'Mother, those days are gone,' Giles said quietly. 'Westcott himself is a wealthy man and is highly regarded in the neighbourhood.'

'What has that to say to anything?' his mother demanded. 'Much you know about it! India, this is another of your queer starts. I fear you have learned nothing since your marriage. I forbid you to receive her. Isham can know nothing of her background. He has been deceived, which is what I would expect from that sly little madam.'

Giles flushed and was about to speak when he was forestalled.

'Is someone taking my name in vain?' a mild voice enquired.

'Oh, Anthony, there you are, thank heavens! Now will you explain to India that she cannot possibly receive a baker's daughter...this Lady Whitelaw, or whatever she calls herself. I know that this will be a shock to you, but you have been misled. I know that girl, and I would put nothing past her. Lady Whitelaw, forsooth! She was a nursemaid to the family, nothing more.'

'I believe she held that post.' Isham's voice was dangerously quiet, and India closed her eyes. Would her mother never learn? Nothing aroused her husband to anger more quickly than any criticism of his wife.

Mrs Rushford was oblivious of the warning signs. 'Certainly she did, and nothing surprised me more. The girl was fifteen when she ran away from home. Who knows what her life had been before she met the Whitelaws? None of us can be in much doubt, I think. She was always a pert, opinionated miss.'

Isham strolled over to the fireplace. 'You question Lord and Lady Whitelaw's judgement then?' The edge to his voice was lost on Mrs Rushford.

She tossed her head. 'They wouldn't be the first to be taken in by her. She will not have changed. She may claim the title, but I, for one, will be surprised if she has any right to it.'

'Then you must prepare yourself for a shock, Isabel. I was Whitelaw's supporter at their wedding.'

Mrs Rushford stared at him. 'You were? But Anthony, you could not have known about her. How can India receive the daughter of a baker? The scandal will run like wildfire through the Ton. I can't imagine what Lady Wells will have to say.'

'As my wife, India need not concern herself with the opinion of vulgarians. Lady Whitelaw will be received here. I must hope that you will make her welcome.'

Mrs Rushford flushed an unbecoming shade of purple. It was a sharp rebuke, though his lordship had not raised his voice. Her visit to Bristol had caused her to forget just how unpleasant her son-in-law could be when he got on his high ropes. Now he sat down beside his wife and took her hand.

India squeezed it gently and he understood. His lofty manner left him as he turned to her sister.

'So we are to wish you happy, Letty?' His smile transformed the harsh face. 'When is the great day to be?'

'In the summer, Anthony.' Letty was radiant. 'Oliver and I are both so grateful to you. Without your help it could not have come about.'

'Nonsense! Oliver would not have let you go, whatever the difficulties.' Pointedly, he made no reference to the dreaded Lady Wells and Letty did not mention her. Anthony was no hypocrite. If her future mother-in-law had dropped off the face of the planet he would consider it a blessing. She twinkled at him, well aware of his feelings in that respect. Anthony turned back to his wife.

'You are looking better,' he said quietly. 'Has the nausea gone?'

'It is soon over,' she assured him. 'And Lucia has a sovereign remedy. I am to eat a dry biscuit when I wake and drink one of her tisanes.' She blushed a little. 'She says that it will last only for the first few weeks.'

At this moment his stepmother came into the room. Lucia, the dowager Lady Isham, was looking pale and fragile. The loss of her own son had hit her hard, but now she devoted herself to India's welfare.

'Shall you feel able to eat your nuncheon, India?' she asked in her prettily accented English. 'It is so important, my dear one.' She grasped the younger woman's hand and led the way into the dining-room.

Yet it was not India who ignored the food. Giles was too preoccupied to notice what was set before him.

So Gina was a widow? Now, at least, he had no need to picture her in the arms of the elderly Lord Whitelaw. The sense of relief had shaken him to the core, though common-sense persuaded him that it was not much of a comfort. Gina was still beyond his reach. He had nothing to offer her. Had it not been for India's generosity in giving him the management of her estate, he would have been forced to return to a way of life which disgusted him. Since his father's death last summer and the ruin of his family he had been forced to live upon the charity of his friends, accepting invitations to their country houses in the hope that someone would offer him employment.

Napoleon's blockade, the ruin of trade, and a failed harvest had dashed that hope. No one needed an estate manager, however dedicated. Had it not been for India's offer he would have been forced to leave the country and seek his fortune overseas.

Then he took himself to task. He must not be bitter. The Rushford family had survived. India's splendid marriage had seen to that. Soon Letty would be wed to her beloved Oliver. He must be happy for them, ignoring the ache in his own heart.

It would be years before he could think of marriage for himself, though his mother still hoped that he would find a wealthy bride. He would not sell himself. Every instinct revolted at the thought. Perhaps he would never marry, but in time he might recover some of his self-esteem.

His preoccupation didn't go unnoticed. India, surprised by her brother's inattention, looked across at her husband and raised an enquiring eyebrow. Isham smiled, but he gave an imperceptible shake of his head, warning her not to pursue the subject. It was not until later, when she was resting in her room, that he came to her. Sitting beside her on the bed he took her hand and raised it to his lips, kissing her fingers each in turn.

'Well, my love?' he teased. 'Had you not better ask me before you burst with curiosity?'

'You mean about Lady Whitelaw?' she asked artlessly. 'Oh, Anthony, you know that I shall be happy to receive her, or any of your friends...'

'I didn't doubt it, but I wasn't referring to Gina Whitelaw, and well you know it.'

'You still find my face an open book then?' India blushed and then she laughed.

'I do, and It's a lovely face. Now, out with it! You are concerned about your brother, are you not?'

'I can't help it. He is behaving oddly. Have you not noticed? I thought he might have spoken to you.'

Isham was silent as India studied his face.

'He has said something, hasn't he?' she insisted. 'I know that you would not betray a confidence, but Giles is so dear to me. I can't help wondering if something dreadful happened whilst he and Letty were away with Mama.'

Isham laughed aloud. 'Nothing of the sort. Giles is more than capable of dealing with Lady Wells, in the politest possible way, of course. She may be a termagant, but she is no match for him. Besides, are we not much in favour with her ladyship at present, now that Letty is to marry Oliver?'

India shook her head at him. 'Don't try to change the subject, Anthony. You shall not divert me with talk of Letty's wedding.'

His lordship stretched out his long legs and regarded her with a fond smile. 'I didn't expect to do so, my darling.'

'Well then, what else can it be? Mother and Letty have not mentioned anything untoward, but Giles is not himself and it worries me.'

'Now that does concern me.' Isham's smile was gone. 'I won't have it, India!' Swiftly he put his arms about her. 'This should be the happiest of times for us. You are not to worry about Giles, or anything else for that matter. I forbid it! Giles is a man grown, and must be allowed to handle his own affairs. He will not welcome interference in what, I suspect, may be a matter of the heart...'

'Oh, did he say so?' India's frown vanished.

'He did not! And, my clever little witch, you shall not tease me into repeating our conversation. As you say, you and Giles are close. He will tell you if he wishes you to know.'

'Perhaps it was just a lovers' quarrel.' India brightened. 'We had many of those ourselves, if you recall?'

'Shall I ever forget?' His lordship threw his eyes to heaven. 'You left me scarred for life!'

'What nonsense!' India's indignant tone was belied by the sparkle in her eyes. 'You seem to have come about, my lord.'

'Only with difficulty, and much self-mortification.'

As he had hoped, his wife's brow cleared and she began to laugh. 'I haven't seen much sign of that.'

'Then it must have been your kisses which restored me.' He turned her face to his and sought her lips. India submitted willingly, but at last she pushed him away.

'You are a disgrace!' she teased. 'Making love to your own wife in the middle of the afternoon! I never heard of such a thing!'

'You prefer that I made love to someone's else's wife in the middle of the afternoon?'

'Only if you seek further scarring, my dear sir.

Now let us be serious. What are we to do about Giles?'

'Nothing at all, I fear.'

'We might at least find him some diversion. He can't have enjoyed his stay with Lady Wells, although it may be there that he met this mysterious paramour.'

'Quite possibly.' Isham would not be drawn.

'Well, now, at least, he will have some company of his own age. Thomas Newby is visiting Abbot Quincey. He puts up at the Angel. Shall we ask him to stay here?'

'Anything you wish, my dearest.'

A loving smile was his reward. 'He is one of my brother's oldest friends...' India paused 'And then, you know, there is Lady Whitelaw...'

Isham kept his countenance with difficulty. 'You also have plans for her, my love?'

India looked a little conscious. 'It is just that... Oh, don't give me that quizzing look, you odious creature... I thought that she might care to dine with us this week.'

'Together with Giles and Thomas Newby? Matchmaking, India?'

'Not at all,' she said severely. 'I thought merely that she might like to bring the girls, so that we may get to know them.'

'Too kind!' His eyes were twinkling and his tone was so dry that she aimed a playful blow at him. 'I'll leave you to rest, my dear, and to do your plotting in peace.'

Having satisfied himself that India was no longer

so deeply troubled, Isham returned to the salon. There he found Letty and Mrs Rushford absorbed in the details of Letty's trousseau, whilst Giles was anxious to slip away.

'I must return to Abbot Quincey,' Isham announced mendaciously. 'Giles, will you ride in with me?'

His brother-in-law gave him a look of relief. 'I'd be glad to, but I feel that I ought to see the bailiff. There must be matters to attend…'

'Time enough for that,' Isham told him firmly. 'We can discuss them as we go.' He rang the bell to order the horses saddled and brought round.

As they set off Giles turned to him and smiled. 'Thanks for coming to my rescue. For these past few days I have heard of nothing but the latest fashions and the merits of Brussels lace against that of Nottingham. I know nothing of such matters, so it was useless to appeal to me.'

Isham laughed. 'Best make up your mind to it, my dear fellow. For the ladies this will be the main topic of conversation until Letty is wed. Just grin and bear it. A man can do nothing else.'

Giles nodded. 'Is all well with the estate? I'd hoped to try some of the newest farming methods this year. Pray heaven we get a better harvest. These last few years have been a disaster on the land.'

'You've done your best in impossible circumstances.' Isham did not elaborate. Both he and his companion were aware that Gareth Rushford had been a drain upon the family's resources for more years than his son could remember. 'I like your ideas.

Perhaps you'll give me the benefit of your expertise on some of my other properties?'

Such praise warmed the heart of his companion. Giles was a countryman to the core. He kept abreast of all the latest developments in agriculture, taking note of any innovations which might be of use to him.

Now he flushed with pleasure, but feeling slightly embarrassed he was quick to change the subject.

'You must have much upon your mind,' he said. 'Have you news from London? We were rather out of touch at Bristol.'

Isham frowned. 'The riots in the north have spread, and the Government won't hear of moderation. I voted against the Framebreakers' Bill, but it was passed. Even Byron spoke out against it in his maiden speech, but to no effect.'

'Byron?' Giles looked surprised. 'I always thought him a frippery sort of fellow.'

'So did I, but he was clear that repression was not the answer. "Can you commit a whole country to their own prisons? Will you erect a gibbet in every field and hang men up like scarecrows?" he asked. I could only agree with him.'

'Even though Henry was killed by the rioters?'

'Even so. Starving men should not be executed and transported when they try to save their livelihood. The means they chose were violent, but they were in a desperate plight, and the Government ignored them.'

'Byron continues with the struggle?'

'Alas, no! He is lionised everywhere since the publication of his epic poem. The women leave him no time for ought but dalliance.'

'Have you read it?' Giles began to smile.

'I tried,' Isham replied with feeling. 'I must be lacking in sensibility, but these gothic flights of fancy are not to my taste.'

'And India?'

'India cannot understand the fuss about *Childe Harold's Pilgrimage*. For that I must be grateful. Poor William Lamb has lost his wife to the fellow. The scandal has London by the ears.'

'Shall you go up again quite soon?'

'I must appear for the reading of the Catholic Bill. Wellesley resigned on the matter a couple of months ago. He doesn't believe in emancipation.'

Giles looked blank. 'Oh, I thought it was because of the Government's support of the Peninsular war.'

'That too. The last we heard was that Wellington was planning to take Badajoz. Let us hope that he is successful. We need a victory.'

Still discussing the conduct of the war in Spain, the two men rode along until they reached the outskirts of the village. Then Isham changed the subject.

'Your friend Tom Newby puts up at the Angel,' he remarked. 'He sent yesterday to ask for you. We'd be happy to have him stay at the Grange if you care to ask him.'

'Oh, would you? How good you are! He is the best of fellows, and I stayed with him last summer. But…er…will it not be too much for India to have a visitor in the house?'

'It will not!' Isham replied firmly. 'The staff know better than to trouble her with domestic details. They do so at their peril.'

Giles grinned. 'I don't doubt it. Well, then, if you are sure, I'll stop by at the Angel and speak to Tom. He's something of a rattle-pate, but I won't let him tire her.'

'She'll enjoy a change of company.' With this assurance Isham raised a hand in salute and rode off to keep his fictitious appointment. In the event, he turned into his favourite bookshop in search of the latest novels for his wife.

Giles had no difficulty in finding Thomas Newby. That gentleman was seated comfortably in the snug, toasting himself by a roaring fire and addressing a tankard of ale with every appearance of enjoyment.

'There you are, old chap!' Thomas hailed his friend with a beaming smile. 'I made sure you'd look me up as soon as you got back from…Bristol…was it not?'

'It was.' Giles raised a finger to summon the landlord. 'Ever been there, Newby?'

'Not that I recall. A seaport, ain't it, full of slaves and tobacco?' Having given Giles the benefit of his scant knowledge of geography Thomas sought further information. 'Lively, is it and full of pretty wenches?'

'I have no idea,' Giles said drily. 'Young Wells and my sister Letty were the only young company and they had eyes only for each other. An engagement, you see. I spent my time playing cards with the dowagers…'

Thomas whistled in surprise. 'Dangerous! Some of those old biddies spend their lives at cards. They could teach the faro-dealers a thing or two. Did they clean you out?'

Giles gave him a wry grin. 'Unlikely…at a penny a point…!'

Thomas shook his head. 'Dear old chap! How did you stand the excitement?'

'It wasn't easy!' The humour of the situation struck Giles suddenly and both men roared with laughter.

'That's better! You looked a bit down, old fellow.' Thomas was too much of a gentleman to pry into his friend's private affairs. 'How goes the world with you these days? Heard you were managing an estate.'

'It belongs to my sister. By the way, she asks if you would care to stay with us. You'll like her. India is a great gun, and Letty too. India married Isham last December. I expect you heard of it. Do you know him?'

'I know *of* him.' Thomas said carefully. 'Always thought him a bit above my touch.'

'So did I. At first I was against the match, but I was wrong. He's made my sister as happy as a grig. I think him the best of men.'

'That's good enough for me. I'll be happy to accept your invitation.' Thomas rang for the landlord and ordered his bags brought down.

'Fine country this,' he observed as they rode towards the Grange. 'Is it good farming land?'

It was enough to launch Giles into his favourite subject, and Thomas was content. He'd seen from the first that Giles had something on his mind. He had little knowledge of agriculture, but beneath his clowning he was a kindly man.

Over the years he'd been aware of his friend's struggles. He's just had one blow too many, he thought to himself. It's time he had some fun.

With this end in mind he felt it time to make some enquiries.

'Much to do round here?' he asked casually.

'I promise you won't be bored.' Giles smiled. 'We can offer you good fishing. Have you read *The Compleat Angler*?'

'Books ain't much in my line, but I did just glance at it. The old chap, Walton, seemed to know his stuff.'

'He did indeed. His river, the Dove, is further to the north, but there is some good sport here.'

'And Abbot Quincey? I must say, I liked the look of it.'

'Or was it the wenches who took your fancy?'

Thomas took the teasing in good part. 'Give me time! I didn't arrive until yesterday, but bless me if I didn't see three beauties driving through the town this morning.'

'I'm surprised that you didn't stop the coach to introduce yourself.'

'It was going too fast, old son. Gave me no time to pull on my boots.'

'Your man isn't with you then?'

'Gave him the slip in London. If there is one thing guaranteed to take the shine off any expedition it's that old curmudgeon, Stubbins. I'm sure my father makes him dog my heels to keep me on the straight and narrow.'

'Has he had much success?' Giles was laughing openly.

'Not that you'd notice.' Thomas gave him a cheerful grin. 'Still, it don't stop him from trying. That's the trouble with people who've known you since before you were breeched. They won't believe you've left the schoolroom.'

'Won't he worry about your disappearance?'

'Stubbins? Not a chance! That fellow is a human bloodhound. He'll track me down before the week is out.'

'Then you'd best make the most of your freedom whilst you may.'

'I intend to,' Thomas said with feeling. 'Now tell me about Abbot Quincey. Is it a big place?'

'It's the largest of our local villages—more like a small market town.' Giles cast a sly look at his friend. 'For your entertainment we have a corn and cattle market on a Tuesday…'

'Wonderful!'

'We also have an abbey and a vicarage…'

'Too much…!'

'Aha, but we also have a scandal. The Abbey is owned by the Marquis of Sywell…'

'What, that old roué…?'

'The same! Now his young wife has disappeared. She hasn't been seen for months. Rumours have been rife. A favourite is that he murdered her.'

'Wouldn't put it past him.'

'It's more likely that she simply ran away.'

'Sounds a reasonable thing to do. Tell me more…'

'No more is known. We *have* had a murder though.'

Thomas looked startled. 'What lives you lead in the quiet of the countryside! I thought that nothing happened here…'

'This came very close to home. Isham's half-brother was killed some weeks ago in one of the Luddite riots. The mob attacked the Grange.'

Thomas reined in at once. 'My dear chap! Have your wits gone a-wandering? The family won't wish for a guest at such a time. I'll go back to the Angel.'

'No, hear me out!' Giles reined in beside his friend. 'There was something strange about the business. Isham and India have said very little, although they saw the shooting.'

'Not a pleasant thing to remember.'

'No, I agree, but I get the feeling that there was more to it than they'll admit. It's an odd affair, and even Henry's mother, who lives with us, seems not to wish to speak of him. It turns out now that he was no blood kin to Isham, though he thought he was.' Giles paused. 'I wish I could explain. It is the strangest thing, but you'll find no sense of mourning at the Grange.'

'Even after such a tragedy?' Thomas was unconvinced.

'You shall see for yourself. Of course, Isham doesn't plan to entertain in his usual style. He isn't much for convention, nor is India stuffy, but you understand?'

'Perfectly. Got to show respect for the dead, old son.'

'Exactly, but even so, you won't be short of company.' Giles allowed the ghost of a smile to touch his lips. 'I have seven cousins in the neighbourhood, and five of them are girls...'

Thomas brightened at the thought of some feminine company. 'Unattached, I hope?'

'As yet. The younger ones are barely out of the schoolroom, but there, you won't mind that. You'll just about be on their level.'

This gibe caused Thomas to aim a playful blow at his companion, which Giles avoided with ease. Spurring his horse ahead, he took off at a gallop across the flat land leading to the Grange.

As Thomas was about to follow, three riders came up fast behind him. As they swept past he decided to give chase. Bruising horsewomen, he thought to himself, but darned if I'll be beaten by three females.

He was well mounted and he caught them up with ease just as their leader swung round to her right and came to a sudden halt.

'What do you want?' a clear voice called. 'I'm armed, so pray don't think of robbing us.'

Thomas swept off his hat. 'My apologies, ma'am. I didn't mean to frighten you.'

'Nor did you do so.' The lady's hand was hidden in the folds of her riding skirt, but a look at her eyes convinced him that it held a pistol. 'Are you in the habit of chasing females, sir?'

'Only pretty ones,' Thomas answered audaciously.

The lady chuckled. 'I phrased that badly, didn't I? What I meant to ask was why you followed us?'

'Ma'am, your speed was irresistible. I can never turn down a race, can you?'

'Not often. Now, sir, tell me who you are. Are we on your land?'

'No, ma'am, but if it were mine you would be more than welcome. My name is Thomas Newby, and I shall be staying at the Grange with Lord and Lady Isham. Are you a stranger to these parts?'

'No, though I have been away for many years. My name is Gina Whitelaw, and these are my stepdaughters, Mair and Elspeth.'

'Why, you are the ladies who were driving past the Angel earlier today,' Thomas exclaimed with delight. 'You looked so charming. Giles said that I should have stopped your coach to introduce myself.'

'Did he indeed?' Gina permitted herself a faint smile. 'I think he could not have known our names.'

'Why no, but he'll be glad to meet you. Here he comes now...'

Giles had turned his horse and was trotting back towards them with a smile of amusement on his lips. He cast a merry eye at Thomas, promising that gentleman a roasting later on. Then his gaze fell upon the ladies and he reined in sharply, causing his mount to rear at the sudden check.

His efforts to control the animal took him several

minutes, much to Thomas's astonishment. His friend's horsemanship was legendary. Now Giles was making much of the simplest of manoeuvres.

It served. By the time he had stilled his restive mount Giles had schooled his expression to one of polite surprise.

'Lady Whitelaw?' he said stiffly. 'Isham told us that you had returned to Abbot Quincey. I…we…had not expected to find you riding out so soon.' He stole a careful look at Gina's face.

He'd dreamed of this moment for so long, wondering how she would react if ever they should meet again. Now he was baffled. In her look he saw no trace of embarrassment, regret, or the least trace of affection.

She gave him a cheerful smile. 'Giles Rushford! What a pleasure it is to see you again! Girls, do you remember Mr Rushford? We met him in Italy long ago.' She might have been greeting a distant acquaintance.

His own heart was pounding at the sight of his lost love. Lost indeed! This sophisticated, self-possessed young woman bore no resemblance to the loving, innocent girl he'd left so long ago.

Chapter Three

'You know each other?' Thomas beamed with pleasure. 'Good! Giles, will you assure her ladyship that I am not a highwayman?'

'My good sir, I didn't think you were.' Gina gave him a demure look. 'Your face was a study when I threatened you with my pistol.'

'I expect it was, ma'am. For all I knew you might have shot first and asked questions afterwards, perhaps in a fright, you see.'

'Gina is never frightened, Elspeth told him proudly. 'She killed two men in India, when they came to rob us.'

'I don't doubt it.' Thomas pretended to cower away, much to the delight of both the girls. 'I'm hoping not to make a third. In a fight, your ladyship, I shall wish to have you on my side...'

'And will you be behind me or in front of me, Mr Newby?'

This sally even brought a smile from Giles, though he felt obliged to offer a word of warning.

'I see that you ride without your groom,' he said. 'Is that wise, Lady Whitelaw? You may not have heard of it , but there is some disaffection in the countryside.'

'Luddites?' Gina gave him a measured look. 'I have no plans either to set up a factory or to import the new machinery, Mr Rushford. The frame-breakers have no quarrel with me.'

'Other elements have joined them,' he told her brusquely. 'The riots have often been a cover for robbery and even murder.'

'I thank you for your concern, but, as you see, I am well armed. As for my groom, he rode ahead of us with a message for your sister. I think I see him in the distance…' Gina was smiling, but there was an edge to her tone which left both men with little doubt that she would brook no interference.

She turned her mount as the groom rode up, and bidding the girls to follow she rode off with a final word of farewell.

Thomas gazed after her with an open mouth.

'That's quite a woman,' he said with feeling. 'Did you see her face when you tried to warn her? That one won't stand quietly in harness for any man.'

'I see no merit in being foolhardy,' Giles retorted.

'Perhaps not, but you won't deny her courage. Do you believe that she killed two men?'

'Oh yes! Isham told me something of her history. She and her family travelled widely, as Whitelaw hoped always to find some cure for his first wife's illness. Gina dealt with a Lascar mutiny on board ship and stood up to the Voodoo priests in the Caribbean…'

'Great heavens! How can you think her foolhardy? I should imagine that she will find no difficulties in this country. Perhaps it is no wonder that her husband lets her ride abroad without protection.'

'She has no husband. Gina is a widow,' Giles said shortly. 'Whitelaw died two years ago.'

'Ah, now I understand. The girls are not her own? I thought her too young to be their mother.'

'Gina has no children of her own, I believe.' Giles urged his horse into a trot, clearly anxious to dismiss the subject, but Thomas could not contain his curiosity.

He stole a look at his friend's face.

'You don't like her, do you? Why is that? I thought her a charming little creature…'

'You think all women charming creatures until they let you down. What happened to that stunning bird of paradise who won your heart last year?'

'I ran out of the dibs, old son. Carriages and jewels cost a mint, to say nothing of that pretty little house in Mayfair. When Brande came along with all his shekels I didn't stand a chance.'

'Shall you go up to London for the Season?'

'Not this year. My father has refused to stand for it. Can't say that I'll miss it much. Stale sandwiches and weak lemonade at Almacks', and dodging all those match-making mamas. Of course if I married the old man would stump up, but what a price to pay!'

'You are incorrigible!'

'I know it. But women are funny creatures, aren't

they? They won't rest until they have you by the leg, and then they try to change you, Won't do for me. I plan to remain a bachelor, and you, for one, won't argue with that.'

If this was an invitation to a confidence Giles ignored it. How could he explain that he longed for nothing more than to make Gina his wife?

True, she had changed, but perhaps no more than he himself. Behind the elegance and the casual politeness of a woman of the world there was still the same indomitable spirit. Her smile, the turn of her head and her graceful carriage reminded him so vividly of the days when he had held her to his heart, murmuring endearments and secure in the knowledge that she returned his love.

It all seemed so long ago, and clearly the years of their separation had killed that love once and for all. He could not blame her. He too had changed. At thirty he was no longer a carefree youth prepared to conquer the world for his lady's pleasure. The years of struggle had taken their toll.

He would not, could not, ask her to wait till he might offer her a comfortable future. Gina would marry again, he was sure of it. She was made for love. Why should she waste her youth in vain hopes, even if he should manage to win back her affections. Better to put it out of his mind and pray that when she did re-marry he was not around to witness it.

Gina herself was taking a much more sanguine view of matters. She had been half dreading meeting

Giles again, unsure of her ability to hide her feelings for him. Now the first hurdle had been overcome and she was pleased with the result. She had had long experience in keeping her countenance. What she could not control was the thudding of her heart. To her it had seemed deafening. Surely he must have heard it?

'Gina, you were unkind to Giles,' Elspeth accused. 'Why did you call him Mr Rushford? I thought he was a friend of ours.'

'He used to be,' Gina said carefully. 'But that was long ago...'

'But you told us that once a friend, always a friend,' Elspeth persisted.

'So I did, but times and people change. When we knew Mr Rushford he was just a boy, and you were babies. Perhaps he has forgotten the days when you used to play together.'

'No, he hasn't.' Mair spoke with conviction. 'He looked so sad. I wanted to make him smile.'

'And you will do so, my dear one.' Gina gathered her charges to her. 'I have a surprise for you. Lord and Lady Isham have invited us to dine with them.'

'Oh, Gina, are we to go as well, even though we are not out?'

'This is just a small family party, my dears, and I have no fears for you. You know how to behave. It is so much more sensible to learn how to conduct yourselves in company before you are thrown headlong into a London season.'

'Darling Gina!' Both girls hugged her. 'We shall be very good. You'll be proud of us…'

The excitement of being invited to dine at the Grange lasted for the next few days and led to long discussions as to suitable toilettes, and who was likely to be their dinner partners.

'I shall hope to be seated by Mr Newby,' Elspeth announced artlessly. 'Giles is much more handsome, of course, but Mr Newby is my idea of a perfect gentleman.'

This brought cries of amusement from Gina and Mair.

'Don't tell me that Lord Isham is no longer your idol,' Gina teased.

'Well, Mair was right. He is a little old for me. Besides he is married now…'

'For all you know Mr Newby may be married too,' Mair said wickedly.

'Oh, I don't think so. He has not the look of a married person…'

'And what look is that?' Gina was vastly amused.

'Oh, I don't know…perhaps I mean a little staid.'

'Like me?' Gina enquired.

Her companions shouted with glee. 'Not in the least like you,' said Mair.

'Of course not.' Elspeth was quick to support her sister. 'You are no more staid than Mr Newby. Isn't he fun? He makes me laugh so much.'

'I see that he is a paragon of all the virtues. You are quite sure that you were not swayed by his compliments?'

'Of course not!' Elspeth was indignant. 'I know that gentlemen are trained to make pretty speeches. They don't always mean what they say.'

'It might be as well to remember that...' Gina's smile hid an anxious heart. Who had learned better than she to place no faith in pretty speeches?

When Giles had vanished all those years ago the shock had left her reeling. How many times had she relived those final hours together when they had strolled on the terrace of the villa hand in hand, stopping now and then for a passionate kiss as the moon sailed high above the Mediterranean in a cloudless sky. A silver pathway on the mirror-like surface of the sea had seemed to point the way to a lifetime of happiness and love.

The prospect of a few days apart was little to be regarded when they had all their lives ahead of them. With a final, lingering kiss Gina parted from her love with a promise to see him when her employers should return from a brief trip into the countryside.

That trip was soon cut short. With the breaking of the Treaty of Amiens the French were quickly on the move again as Napoleon resumed his dream of conquest. The whole of Italy was thrown into turmoil. The Whitelaws fled back to their villa on the coast and from there to Naples. Refugees had taken almost every berth on the few available ships. Given no choice Sir Alastair had embarked his family on a merchantman bound for the Caribbean.

Gina had suffered agonies of mind, but Giles was nowhere to be found, and in the panic and confusion of those final days in Italy she had no hope of tracing him. She would not believe him a coward who would take care of his own skin, leaving his friends to fend for themselves.

She'd heard that all foreigners had been advised to leave the country, but he must have had time to send a message to the villa.

She could not know it, but Giles had done so. A frantic message from his uncle had warned him to get out of Italy fast before escape became impossible. His father's affairs were in a bad case and Giles was needed at home.

He'd scrawled a few lines before embarking on a vessel bound for Dublin, but it had taken a heavy bribe to persuade his Italian servant to carry his letter to the Whitelaw's home to await Gina's return. *En route* his messenger had had second thoughts. Why should he risk his neck for what could only be some trivial billet-doux? The man tossed the note into some bushes and turned back to the port, thankful to see that Giles had already sailed. His ship was far out in the bay.

Gina's heart was breaking, but she'd been given no time to mourn. The stress of the enforced evacuation from her home had affected Lady Whitelaw's already fragile health. Gina's days were spent in a whirl of caring for the invalid and cherishing her two small charges. Each night her pillow was wet with tears, but by day her expression gave no hint of her anguish.

Now, after all these years, she realised that the experience would stand her in good stead. No one must be allowed to guess that she still loved Giles.

She'd tried to crush that love, telling herself that he was faithless and that his promises were false. She'd even tried to hate him, but such a destructive emotion was alien to her character. Instead, she'd attempted to banish all thought of him from her mind.

Sometimes it worked. Then some remark, some fragment of a song, would bring her memories flooding back, often just as she was beginning to congratulate herself that the pain was growing less. It was in vain.

Then she would throw herself into a flurry of activity, studying the history of each place to which they travelled, noting the customs of the country, attempting to learn the language, and even to record their expeditions with her modest attempts at painting.

After a few years she didn't often permit herself the indulgence of looking back. What was done was done. She could not change it, nor must she waste the rest of her life in vain regrets. Just as the girls developed, so did Gina. Now, at the age of twenty-six, she was no longer the child who had offered her love so freely. She had learned to face reality, and she'd discovered that life was a mixture of triumphs and disappointments. What mattered, she'd decided long ago, was how you faced them.

This philosophy had served her well. She'd had no hesitation in marrying Sir Alastair after the death of his wife. She loved him dearly, though not as she had loved Giles. Sir Alastair was her closest friend, and she'd known how highly he regarded her.

It was not until Lord Isham had married India Rushford that she had news of her lost love. Then she learned that Giles had never taken a bride, although sometimes she had pictured him with children of his own.

Perhaps it was not too late to find happiness the second time around. Giles was living close to Abbot Quincey, her own birthplace. Swiftly she made plans to move there from the Whitelaw estate in Scotland. She had the perfect excuse. Sir Alastair's daughters were growing up. In a year or two she must give each of them a Season, and Abbot Quincey was not too far from London.

She summoned Anthony Isham to her aid. It was he who had found the ideal house in the centre of the village. Next year she would ask him to suggest a suitable place in town.

Meantime her plan of campaign was working well. She'd been undeceived by her former lover's stiff manner. Gina was not lacking in perception and she'd sensed at once that Giles was far from happy. Mair had been right. His eyes were sad and the tracery of lines upon his brow had almost broken her heart. Even so, he was still the handsomest man she had ever seen. The blond hair might have darkened a little, but nothing could alter the wonderful bone structure of his face, and that brilliant blue gaze still had the power to make her tremble.

But Gina knew her man. This would be no matter

of simply resuming a former love affair. Now their roles were reversed.

When they met Gina had been a servant, and worse, the daughter of the local baker in Abbot Quincey. They'd known the difficulties ahead of them. A gentleman would be shunned by society if he married beneath him.

Now Gina had a title and a handsome fortune. That obstacle had been removed, but there was a greater one. The Rushford family had suffered a great reversal of fortune, saved only by India's marriage to Lord Isham. Giles himself had nothing but his position as India's estate manager.

Even if he still loved her, Gina knew that his own pride would make it impossible for him to offer for her. A match with a wealthy bride might be considered desirable by the Ton, but her own heart told her that he would have none of it. That was unless...unless she could persuade him otherwise.

But how was she to do it? The problem exercised her constantly. Certainly she would not throw herself into his arms. Even if he longed to do so, he would not respond. For the time being she must go slowly, treating him in a friendly way as an old acquaintance and giving him no hint that she remembered what had been between them.

Her first opportunity to carry out this plan came at the Ishams' dinner party. Gina had dressed with care in a favourite gown of cream silk crêpe which she had bought in India. It was trimmed with tiny pearls and with it she wore an overdress of lace.

'Gina, you look positively splendid!' cried Mair. 'You are putting us in the shade.'

'Nonsense! You both look charming. Elspeth, would you like to wear my necklace of river pearls? Mair may have this ornament for her hair.'

'Pearls too!' Simple as the jewels were, the girls preened themselves, reconciled to the fact that they were both in the simplest of white dresses.

Gina smiled at them. 'We'll do,' she teased. 'At the very least we won't frighten the horses.'

They were still laughing as they set off for the Grange, but as they drew closer Mair grew silent.

Gina was quick to sense it. 'What is it, darling?' she asked.

'I shan't be able to think of anything to say,' Mair whispered in despair. 'They'll all think me stupid.'

'Not a bit of it! Ask them about themselves. After that you won't need to say another word of your own, but you'll gain the reputation of a brilliant conversationalist.'

'That's an unkind thing to say.' Mair began to laugh. 'I'm sure it isn't true!'

'Try it!' Gina advised. 'The most absorbing topics of interest for most people are their own concerns.'

'Gina, are you what is known as a cynic?' Elspeth enquired.

'No, darling, just a realist.' Gina picked up her wrap as the carriage drew to a halt, and led the way into the house.

As she walked into the salon followed by the girls

there was a hush. Then India came towards her with a welcoming smile.

'I don't propose to treat you as a stranger, Lady Whitelaw,' she said quickly. 'Welcome home to Abbot Quincey. We are all so glad to see you again, are we not, Mama?'

Mrs Rushford had had much to think about in the past few days. If the former Gina Westcott was now as wealthy as Lord Isham had suggested, it would be the height of folly to ruin the chances of her only son with an ill-timed fit of pique. Besides, she dared not snub the girl or attempt to quell her pretensions with Isham's eyes upon her.

She came forward holding out her hands. 'Little Gina!' she said in sentimental tones. 'Who would have thought that you would come back to us as Lady Whitelaw?'

'Not many people, I imagine, ma'am.' Gina affected not to see the outstretched hands. 'May I present Mair and Elspeth to you? They are my step-daughters.'

'Charming…charming…and scarce more than children, Lady Whitelaw…' Mrs Rushford was about to give her views on the unsuitability of allowing young people to dine with their elders, but Gina turned away.

'You will remember my sister, Letty, I think?' India continued.

'Of course. I remember you with pleasure. You were always such a happy child.'

'Letty is even happier now. She has just become engaged to Oliver Wells.'

Gina's felicitations were sincere. As a child growing up in Abbot Quincey she had always liked the Rushford children and their father. They'd been kind to her, unlike their snobbish mother, who'd spoken to her only to administer some sharp rebuke for speaking up too freely when accused of some trivial misdemeanour.

'Anthony you know very well, but this is Mr Thomas Newby, who is our house-guest, and already one of the family.'

Thomas bowed. 'You are too kind. I have already had the pleasure of meeting Lady Whitelaw and her daughters. We met when Giles and I were out riding some few days ago.' He beamed at the girls and won a smile from each of them.

'Giles, you said nothing of this. What a dark horse you are!'

His sister's teasing had no effect on Giles. His formal bow was perfection, but his face was expressionless.

'I see what it is,' India began to laugh. 'Giles fears for his dignity. He knows that you remember him as a grubby lad, forever falling out of trees.'

This brought a smile from the assembled company and Gina turned to the object of their amusement.

'I promise to forget it,' she said lightly. 'There, it is gone, and lost in the mists of time.' She nodded as if to dismiss the subject, and turned back to India.

'I was hoping to offer my condolences to the

Dowager Lady Isham,' she announced. 'Isham has told me that she lost her son. It must have been a great sorrow to her.'

'It hit her very hard,' India agreed. 'Lucia has been very brave, but sometimes she prefers to be alone. Tonight she will dine in her room.'

'I understand.' Gina grew thoughtful. 'For a mother it must be the greatest tragedy in the world. You will give her my good wishes, will you not?'

'So kind, Lady Whitelaw.' Mrs Rushford sat down beside them and heaved a gusty sigh. 'A mother's heart must bleed for her. Should anything happen to my darling Giles I should not want to live. Such a tower of strength as he has been since the loss of my dear husband.' She touched a lace-trimmed handkerchief to her eyes.

'Mama, please don't distress yourself. Did we not promise each other that this was to be a happy occasion? Lady Whitelaw and her daughters will be such an asset to the village.'

'True!' Mrs Rushford gave a brave smile and returned her unsullied handkerchief to her reticule. 'Have you seen your parents yet, my dear?'

'I called at the bakery,' Gina replied in unaffected tones. If it was vulgar to be in trade so be it. She was not ashamed of her background. That, in her eyes, would be an even greater vulgarity. 'My parents are both well, thank you, ma'am.'

'You did not visit the new house? Why, my dear, it is very fine. I declare that I have been hoping this age for an invitation.'

India exchanged a look with her sister, half amused and half irritated by such a bare-faced lie. Mrs Rushford would have considered an invitation from a tradesman as an insult in itself. It would not even have merited a reply.

'You intend to widen your circle of acquaintance, Isabel? A worthy notion…' Isham looked down at his mother-in-law, his dark face alive with amusement.

Mrs Rushford gave him an uncertain glance. Totally devoid of humour herself, she was never sure whether Anthony was being sarcastic or merely funning.

'Naturally,' she replied in a defensive tone. 'We must all move with the times…' In its way this was an admission that the once despised lower classes were beginning to encroach upon the ranks of the aristocracy, but it was a *faux pas* which reduced her companions to silence.

Gina was the first to recover. A lesser woman might have been crushed by the condescending tone of Mrs Rushford's statement, but Gina's lips began to twitch. It was only with an effort that she preserved her countenance, and when she turned to India her eyes were twinkling.

'Lady Isham, I believe that you and your sister attended Mrs Guarding's Academy? Is she still accepting pupils? Mair and Elspeth must finish their education, and I will apply there if you recommend it.'

'Pray don't think of it, Lady Whitelaw.' Mrs Rushford interrupted in an uncompromising tone. 'That woman corrupts young minds. The place should be closed by order of the magistrates. She preaches sedition.'

Lord Isham took a seat beside her with every expectation of enjoyment. 'Strong words, Isabel! Will you not explain?'

'You know my views,' Mrs Rushford retorted. 'She tries to turn her pupils into blue-stockings, filling their heads with nonsense about independence and women's rights. No man wants a pert, opinionated woman to wife.' Her gaze fell upon Gina, who gave her the sweetest of smiles.

'But neither does a sensible man wish for his life-long companion and the mother of his children to be an empty-headed nincompoop,' Giles said hotly.

'Of course not, my dear boy. You misunderstand me. A girl must be trained to be an ornament to society. She must learn to carry herself gracefully, to dress well, to dance, to sing a little, and there can be no objections to lessons in painting and drawing.'

Gina's shoulders were shaking. Her own 'training', such as it was, had been very different, especially as it had included lessons in marksmanship. She had also learnt how to throw a knife. These accomplishments were, however, unlikely to be of use to young ladies brought up in the heart of England.

She raised her head to find that Giles was looking at her. She suspected that, as always, he had read her mind, for his own eyes were dancing. She looked away.

'Mama, we learned those things at Mrs Guarding's

Academy,' Letty protested gently. 'Her teachers were the best that could be found.'

'Some of them, if not others,' her mother said darkly. 'However, I don't propose to indulge in gossip.'

With a valiant effort, India avoided her husband's eye, and also that of Letty, but the tirade wasn't over.

'What, may I ask, is the use of filling a young woman's head with mathematics, and so-called philosophy, which, as I understand it, is simply another name for radical views? It will not help her to run her household or hire and fire her servants.'

'Mrs Guarding seeks merely to teach a girl to use her mind,' India protested. 'The actual subjects do not matter over-much.'

'That's as maybe! That woman has done untold damage. Look at your cousin Hester! She's a constant worry to her parents. And as for that trollop, Desirée Nash, she should be whipped at the cart's tail. Teaching philosophy, Greek and Latin. She'd have taught her pupils more than that if Mrs Guarding hadn't dismissed her.'

India gave a discreet cough to call her mother's attention to the fact that Mair and Elspeth had drifted away from Thomas Newby's side when schooling was mentioned, and were both listening with avid interest to Mrs Rushford's remarks.

It was fortunate that at that moment dinner was announced. With his customary courtesy Isham offered his arm to Mrs Rushford. Thomas Newby es-

corted India and Giles offered an arm to Gina and
Letty.

Gina found herself seated between Giles and Lord
Isham. She had not expected it, and was disturbed to
be so close to her former love. His hand was inches
from her own, and when he reached across her shoulders to help her remove her gauzy scarf his fingers
touched the bare flesh of her neck.

Giles started back as if he'd been stung.

'I beg your pardon,' he muttered.

'Not at all,' Gina replied politely. 'It is kind of you
to help me. Some of these fashions are well enough
in their way, but a scarf is not improved when it falls
into the soup.'

It was not the most sophisticated of remarks. Gina
felt that she was babbling to hide the fact that her
senses were on fire. Her heart was beating wildly, but
she was determined not to betray herself. The long-
practised self-control came to her aid once more. She
turned to Isham.

'What do you think, Anthony? Shall I send the girls
to the Academy?'

'By all means. The standard of teaching is high.
You won't do better for them.' Isham smiled down
at his companion, apparently unaware of the tension
in the air. Yet he had felt it from the first. Gina was
more on edge than he had ever known her. There was
some mystery here.

Chapter Four

'Shall you go up to London for the Season, Lady Whitelaw?' Thomas enquired.

'We've decided to postpone that pleasure until next year, when Mair comes out. Anthony, I hope, will advise us as to a house when the time comes.'

Lord Isham nodded his agreement.

Then Gina was possessed by an imp of mischief. 'Besides,' she said, 'before I go I must learn to waltz…'

'Shocking!' There was a sniff of disapproval from Mrs Rushford. 'Young men careering about a ballroom with ladies in their arms? I must hope that my own girls won't consider it.'

'I'm sorry to hear you say so,' Gina replied solemnly. 'The Prince Regent finds it delightful. In future it will be the rage at all his parties.'

'Which, of course, you will attend, Lady Whitelaw?' There was no mistaking the malicious note in Mrs Rushford's voice.

'Why yes, I believe so, ma'am.' Gina regarded her

questioner with an innocent gaze. 'We are invited to Brighton in September.'

This was enough to reduce Mrs Rushford to silence, and Thomas Newby stepped into the breach.

'When I left town Lady Caroline Lamb was holding waltz parties in the mornings,' he observed to no one in particular. 'It gave me a chance to practice.'

'Truly, can you waltz?' Elspeth was seated beside him, much to her delight. Now she gazed at him with awe.

'I make some kind of a stab at it,' he admitted modestly.

'I don't suppose...I mean...if you came to see us would you show us how it is done?' Elspeth knew that whispering was rude, but she wasn't exactly whispering, was she? She was simply speaking in too low a voice for her words to reach Mrs Rushford's ears.

Thomas replied in the same tone. 'Glad to, Miss Elspeth, if your stepmama don't mind. Got to be up to the mark with the latest fads and fancies, haven't we?'

'Oh, you do understand!' Elspeth gave him a grateful look. 'When one is almost out it is very hard to be treated like a child. Gina doesn't do it, but other people do. I hope she won't insist on sending us to that Academy to finish our education.'

'Well, as I understand it, it isn't a school, Miss Elspeth. It's more like a university for ladies, in a small way, of course.' He smiled. 'It might turn you into a revolutionary.'

Elspeth giggled. 'Are you a revolutionary, Mr Newby?'

'Not I! Don't understand these politician fellows. Always arguing about something, and never getting anything done.' His voice had risen and his words were clearly audible during a pause in the conversation of his fellow guests.

'You are very hard on us, Newby.' Anthony was laughing openly. 'Give us some credit, man. We do try, you know.'

Thomas flushed to the roots of his hair, and he made haste to apologise to his host. 'I didn't mean you, my lord. We know how hard you've worked to ease conditions in the north, and for the machinists here.'

Isham grinned at him. 'So it doesn't all escape you, Mr Newby?'

'I talk to people,' Thomas said vaguely. 'What I know don't come from books, my lord.'

'Many more of us might profit by your example,' Isham replied. 'Sometimes I feel that we foist our ideas on the people, giving them what we think they need, instead of what they want.'

'My dear Anthony! Unlettered louts? Would you have them decide the conduct of the country?' Mrs Rushford could contain herself no longer.

'I thought you believed in a lack of education?' Anthony said mildly. 'Have we not just been discussing the matter?'

'We were speaking of women,' his mother-in-law replied in angry tones.

It was enough to bring India into the conversation with a request to be brought up to date with the London gossip.

'I hope you don't mind,' she said to Gina in a low voice. 'I'll take care to see that nothing untoward reaches the ears of the girls, though Mr Newby will be well aware of the need for discretion in young company.'

She was right. Thomas rose to the occasion. In minutes he had them laughing at the Prince Regent's favourite story.

'Do stop me if you've heard it...' He looked around the table. 'It's the one about the running race.'

'Oh, no! Do tell us!' Elspeth couldn't contain her curiosity, and was rewarded with a look from Mrs Rushford which indicated that young people should be seen and not heard.

'Very well then. This is the story of the fattest man in Brighton. He wagered heavily on himself to win a foot race against the town's best runner.'

'That doesn't sound very sensible...' Gina was smiling as she awaited the outcome of the story.

'He was cunning, ma'am. He made only two conditions. The first was that he should choose the route, and the second was that he should have a ten-yard start. As you can imagine, there were no objections. In fact, he was offered a fifty-yard start, but he didn't take it.'

'The spectators must have thought him mad,' Giles interjected. 'The odds against him winning must have been enormous.'

'They were, but this crafty fellow made a fortune. When the starting pistol was fired he set off down the narrowest streets in Brighton at a jog-trot. His rival came up from behind, but he couldn't pass that vast bulk. Our hero filled the narrow lanes from side to side.'

Even Mrs Rushford was forced to smile. 'Mr Newby, are you acquainted with the Prince?' she asked.

'No, ma'am, my father…er…feels that his fortune would be insufficient to support me in those circles.'

This brought another smile from the assembled company.

'Even so, I'd like to see his palace by the sea,' Thomas admitted. 'I'm told It's like an Oriental seraglio, whatever that is.'

Being well acquainted with the exact meaning of the word, Isham felt it time to step in.

'The Prince refers to his place as a cottage,' he said with some amusement. 'In view of the vast sums lavished on it, it must be the most expensive cottage in the country.'

'Do you like it, Anthony?' Gina was curious.

'It isn't to my taste. I have no quarrel with this fascination for the East and Orientalism. Some of the Prince's treasures are very fine indeed. However, it is difficult to appreciate so many when they fill every room.'

'I hear that he keeps the place at hothouse temperature.' Mrs Rushford was fascinated by this glimpse into the lifestyle of the heir to the throne.

'He does, ma'am, and that, combined with his taste for busy wallpapers and extravagant decoration of every kind, has had a stifling effect on some of his visitors. A lady of my acquaintance described it as "fairly buzzing". It made her feel quite faint.'

'So one must suffer a little if one wishes to hear the Prince sing or conduct the orchestra in his music room?'

'Yes, Gina. You must be prepared for some discomfort when you visit Brighton in September.'

'We shan't mind. I hear he has a pleasant singing voice and reads the poetry of Scott and Southey to perfection. That will please Mair.'

'Your stepdaughter will be in a minority,' Mrs Rushford retorted sharply. 'The Regent is one of the most unpopular men in England with his constant spending, and his disloyalty to his friends, to say nothing of certain other matters.' She glanced significantly at the two young girls. 'As for that poor wife of his…!'

Gina was tempted to ask which wife she had in mind. It was common knowledge that the Prince had gone through some sort of wedding ceremony with his mistress, Mrs Fitzherbert, before his official marriage to the Princess Caroline. His reputation as a bigamist did nothing to enhance his popularity in the country.

'Now, Mama, we know that you champion the Princess's cause, but we must leave the gentlemen to their port…' India rose from the table, anxious to avoid a diatribe about the Regent's treatment of his wife. She herself imagined that there must be faults on both sides, but her mother would not hear of it.

In the salon she rang for tea and called Mair and Elspeth to her. They were favourites with Anthony, and having met them she could understand it.

Elspeth was short and plump, but Mair, with her gazelle-like frame, was unlikely ever to reach the buxom proportions so much admired by society. In her case it would not matter, India thought to herself. There was character in that youthful face. Perhaps the jaw was a little too square, the brow too wide and the mouth too generous for true beauty, but her Celtic origins were apparent in the high cheekbones, the mass of dark hair, and the vivid blue eyes, set off by a perfect skin.

Elspeth was undeniably her sister, but she had not yet lost her puppy fat, and in her, at present, one saw only the energetic schoolgirl.

India began to question them, speaking as she would to an adult. This she'd found was a subtle form of flattery, which never failed to please young people.

'Shall you attend the fête at Perceval Hall?' she asked. 'My aunt would be happy to see you there. She runs these affairs for charity.'

'We haven't heard of it,' Mair told her shyly.

'Oh, of course not. How foolish of me! I had forgot that you had but recently arrived in Abbot Quincey. If you'd like to go I'll ask her to send you an invitation.'

'Oh, would you, Lady Isham?' Elspeth gave her an earnest look. 'Gina will take us, I feel sure of it. What happens at the fête? We didn't have them in Scotland.'

'It's an excuse for a party,' India replied. 'There are all kinds of competitions, such as bobbing for apples, and pinning a tail upon a donkey when one is blindfold. There are races too, with prizes.'

'Horse races?' Elspeth glanced at her sister.

'Horse races, sack races, three-legged races, and ordinary running races. You may take your pick. There are trials of strength, and a tug-of-war, and even an archery competition.'

'It sounds such fun,' Elspeth said warmly. 'Gina will love it.' She glanced across at her stepmother, who was deep in conversation with Letty and Mrs Rushford. 'We'll tell her about it later.'

'Well, don't forget to mention the refreshments and the country-dancing…' India looked up as the gentlemen came to join them. A glance sent Isham to rescue Gina from the cross-questioning she was suffering at the hands of Mrs Rushford.

'Thank heavens for that!' Letty sank on to the couch beside her sister. 'Poor Gina! I don't know how she kept her temper. Mama has almost asked her for details of her fortune…'

'We'll have to put a stop to that. What do you say to a game of cards with Mother? It will keep her out of mischief…' A glance of complicity passed between the sisters. Then India made her suggestion.

It was greeted with enthusiasm by Mrs Rushford, who was quick to choose Anthony as her partner. She'd learned from bitter experience that it was almost impossible to beat him and she preferred to have him on her side. Besides, a plan was forming in her mind.

'Lady Whitelaw will like to see the Orangery,' she told Giles in a tone which brooked no argument. 'India and Letty will make up our table.'

'Lady Whitelaw may prefer to join you,' Giles retorted stiffly.

'My dear boy, five people cannot play, and India must undertake a restful occupation. Letty, as you know, is mad for cards…'

This came as news to Letty, who was too startled to reply. She could not look either at India or at Anthony.

'Mrs Rushford is quite right,' Gina was trying not to laugh. 'I believe I mentioned to her that I have no head for cards. I should be most interested to see the Orangery and the gardens. I shall need advice on how to improve my grounds, so perhaps the gentlemen will give me the names of certain plants, and the girls and I will try to remember them.'

Anthony glanced at his wife, who managed to preserve her countenance only with the greatest difficulty. Her mother's plan had been foiled in the most charming way possible. Mrs Rushford had not envisaged the entire party setting forth into the garden.

Giles was furious with her. Her scheming was all too obvious and it filled him with embarrassment. For two pins he would have walked away, but good manners forced him to lead the party through the Orangery and on to the terrace.

He'd planned to take the girls up to the Folly on the hill, but Thomas was ahead of him. Already a favourite with Mair and Elspeth, that gentleman had been challenged to a race and all three were already disappearing into the distance.

In silence he paced beside Gina, but he couldn't look at her.

'Pray go ahead if you wish to join the others,' Gina told him cheerfully. 'I'm afraid that these flimsy evening slippers are not meant for walking.'

'No! I do *not* wish to join the others.' Suddenly Giles longed to tear aside that polished social veneer. 'Must we pretend that we are strangers?'

Gina gave him a sideways look. 'Of course not! Why should you think that? We knew each other as children, and Anthony knows that we met in Italy. Oh, I see! You feel that you should have mentioned to your family that we'd met since my return to Abbot Quincey? That is not so very dreadful. They did not seem to take it amiss...'

'No, I was not referring to that and well you know it.' Giles stopped suddenly and swung round to face her. 'Look at me!' he demanded. 'I can't pretend that we are casual acquaintances...can you?'

'Most certainly I can,' she replied in level tones. 'I'd advise you to do the same.'

Her companion groaned. 'I don't believe that you have forgotten what we once were to each other.'

'I've not forgotten.' With an effort Gina kept her voice steady. 'But it was long ago. I was younger than

Mair is now. At that age one has little experience of the world, and a childish folly is soon forgotten.'

Giles looked as if she had struck him. Until today he'd been resolved that he would never remind her of their love, but his good resolutions had deserted him.

Quickly, he pulled himself together. 'Even so,' he said. 'I feel I owe you an explanation…'

Gina lifted a dismissive hand. 'You owe me nothing…'

'No, please hear me out. I didn't know where to find you. Why didn't you answer my letter?'

'What letter?' she demanded. 'I received no letter.'

Giles stared at her in stupefaction. 'I wrote to you before I sailed…before you came back to the villa. It was to tell you why I'd had to leave so quickly.'

'There was nothing,' she told him.

'Damn the fellow! I paid him well to carry the message.' Giles turned his face away. 'What you must of thought of me?'

'It *was* difficult to understand,' she admitted. 'I hadn't supposed you to be a man who would flee at the first sign of danger, but conditions in Naples were chaotic. Before I knew it we were *en route* to the West Indies.'

'You could have written to me at the Grange,' he said miserably.

'I suppose so, but we were always on the move. It wasn't easy to find a ship prepared to carry mail.' She wouldn't tell him that she'd been too hurt and also too proud to beg him to come back to her.

'I tried to find *you*, you know. I made enquiries at the bakery until your mother became suspicious. I said that Sir Alastair was a friend of mine and I wondered what had happened to him, but I don't think she believed me.'

'She wouldn't have been able to help you. I wrote to my parents when I could, but if they replied their letters never reached me.'

'Oh, Gina, you must have been so lonely.'

'Sometimes, perhaps, but I had the girls, and Sir Alastair and his wife were always good to me.' Gina managed an engaging smile. 'It is difficult to be sad, you know, when one is embroiled in so much action. Distant countries are always full of interest, but they aren't the safest places in the world.'

'I heard something of your exploits from Anthony.'

'Exaggerated, I fear, though I can fire a pistol with some degree of accuracy. Giles, have we not said enough about my affairs? What of you? How do you go on?'

He had been dreading the question, unwilling to admit even to Gina that the fortunes of his family had been saved only by Anthony's marriage to India. The thought still galled him. True, India was happy, but it might so easily have been different. She'd accepted Lord Isham hating him for the part she believed he'd played in the death of her father and the loss of all their property. Only in these last few months had that hatred turned to love.

She'd been prepared to sacrifice herself for his sake, and that of his mother and sister. He could not forget it. Feelings of frustration threatened to over-whelm him. It should have been he who saved the family, and he'd been unable to do so.

It hadn't been for want of trying. Ever since he'd been summoned back from Italy all those years ago he'd been forced to shoulder burdens apparently be-yond the capabilities of a young man.

And he'd almost succeeded in turning the Rushford Estate into a paying proposition. He'd worked day and night to bring it round. Their lands were rich and fertile and he'd immersed himself in study of all the latest farming methods, new thinking on the rotation of crops, new strains of various seeds, and all the latest breeds of cattle.

He'd yearned to have the means to buy those im-plements which would have saved on time and labour, but they were beyond him. Undaunted, he'd been forced to improvise for himself, ignoring the tradi-tional resistance to change so prevalent among all ag-ricultural labourers.

But the drain on his resources had been impossible to halt. Money set aside for improvements had gone to pay the debts of his lovable but feckless father. The end had come last year when, in a night of mad-ness, Gareth Rushford had gambled away the last of his inheritance, losing it to Anthony Isham, and leav-ing his family destitute.

The shock had been severe. Forced to leave her home, his mother had moved into a small cottage owned by her brother-in-law, Sir James Perceval, tak-ing her daughters with her.

Giles himself had travelled the country looking for employment. It had been in vain. Only now, as India's estate manager, could he see some glimmer of hope for the future. He was realistic enough to know that he had years of struggle ahead of him. Far better to forget his one and only love.

He turned away as they caught up with the others and offered to take them to see a badger sett. Gina declined on the grounds that her slippers were quite soaked through in the long grass. She turned back towards the house, with Thomas Newby as her escort.

'Ma'am, we have been thoughtless.' Gallantly, he offered her his arm. 'I must hope that you will not take a chill.'

'Highly unlikely, Mr Newby. It pains me to admit it, but I enjoy the best of health. Such a trial when it is so much more interesting to be always swooning, or in a state of delicate health.'

'Ma'am, you are making game of me.' Thomas grinned at her. 'You would not care to be in such case, I believe.'

'No, I should not.' Companionably Gina tucked her hand into the crook of his arm. 'There is so much enjoyment in this world. One cannot see it from a sofa.'

'Shall you settle in Abbot Quincey, ma'am?' Thomas felt as though he'd known her all his life.

'I don't know yet, Mr Newby. I must consider the girls. Fortunately we are not so far from London here in Abbot Quincey. I may open the London house this year, or possibly in the spring.'

'You speak of the girls. What of yourself?' As he spoke he wondered if she would regard the question as too personal, but she gave him a friendly smile.

'I never make arrangements too far ahead. That way I am not disturbed if I have to change my plans…'

'Very wise. Oh, Lord!' Thomas had caught sight of a horseman in the distance. 'I hope I won't have to change mine. Here comes Stubbins, if I'm not mistaken…'

'Stubbins?'

'My valet, ma'am, or groom, or whatever you like to name him. In reality, he is a watchdog. My father sets him on me…'

'Leave him to me!' Gina's eyes were dancing. She was prepared to enjoy the coming confrontation.

As the man drew rein beside them she moved even closer to her companion.

'Now how did you find me, Stubbins?' Thomas sounded exasperated.

''T'wern't difficult, Mr Thomas. You left a trail a mile wide.'

'Good gracious, Mr Newby,' Gina simpered. 'Are you fleeing from the law?'

'No, ma'am, this is my valet, Stubbins.'

Gina turned a soulful gaze upon the servant. 'Why, Mr Newby will be so glad to see you. He has been sadly at a loss, have you not, my dear?'

Thomas choked and turned his laughter into a cough. 'I have indeed. Where have you been, you dog?'

Stubbins gave his charge an uncertain look. He'd expected fury, defiance and anything but to find his master escorting a lady who would clearly have gained the approval of Mr Newby, senior.

Now Stubbins sought to rally his forces.

'Beg pardon, Mr Thomas, but you left London without giving me your direction…'

'An oversight,' Thomas asserted stoutly.

'Were you thinking of me, my dear?' Gina draped herself artistically about her companion's person. 'How sweet of you.'

Thomas patted her on the shoulder. 'There, there!' he said. 'I must get you back to the Grange before you catch a chill. Stubbins will ride ahead for us. Lady Whitelaw's feet are wet. She must have hot broth as soon as she arrives.' With a wave of his hand he dismissed the dreaded Stubbins. Then he shouted with laughter.

'Mr Newby, please! You must not let him hear you. I'm sure he has your best interests at heart.'

'Now, ma'am, you shall not preach to me. What a card you are! Stubbins will be convinced that I am trying to fix my interest with you. My father will have the news before the week is out.'

'Oh dear!' Gina looked repentant. 'Shall you mind very much? I'm sorry, but Stubbins looked so…so very disapproving of you. I could not resist the opportunity to tease.'

'Lady Whitelaw, from now on you may consider me your slave. I had not thought to live to see the day when Stubbins could be routed.'

'It was unkind of me. You see, Mr Newby, I am not at all to be trusted. I am inclined to follow impulse.'

'And a most charming impulse, ma'am, if I may say so. I am deeply honoured.'

'Come now, Mr Newby,' Gina spoke in a rallying tone. 'We hear on all sides that you are a confirmed bachelor.'

'Lady Whitelaw, you could change my mind,' came the swift reply.

Apparently Gina did not hear him as she went indoors.

Mrs Rushford looked up eagerly as they returned to the salon. Then her face clouded.

'Where is Giles?' Her tone was sharp. She had expected to see Gina escorted by her son and not by Thomas Newby.

'Why, ma'am, he kindly offered to show the girls a badger sett,' Gina told her smoothly. She'd seen the look of mortification on Mrs Rushford's face, and was aware of the reason for it.

'Such folly! Your girls will take their death of cold to be kept outdoors of an evening. I am surprised that you allowed it, Lady Whitelaw. Sometimes I wonder at Giles…so little regard for other people's health…to say nothing of the proprieties!'

'Why, Isabel, what can you mean?' Lord Isham laid his cards aside. 'I hope you aren't suggesting that Mair and Elspeth are in danger of injuring their reputations by taking a walk with Giles.' He gave his mother-in-law a pleasant smile, but she was quick to notice that it did not reach his eyes.

'Of course not!' she said hastily. 'But Giles is so impulsive. Believe me, Lady Whitelaw, he is all heart. It would not occur to him that he might overtire the girls, in his wish to give them pleasure.'

'I thank you for your concern, but the girls are used to walking. As you see, they have come to no harm…' She looked up as the others returned. 'Did you see the badgers?' she enquired.

'We were too early, Gina. They come out to feed only when it is full dark, so Giles tells us…'

Mrs Rushford was silent. It had occurred to her for once that she must watch her tongue, if Gina was to be persuaded into accepting Giles. It could serve no useful purpose to criticise him in public.

That worthy resolution did not apply to a private talk. She called Giles over to her under the cover of general conversation.

'What are you about?' she hissed. 'Must you pay so much attention to those stupid girls? You should be trying to fix your interest with their stepmother.'

Giles paled so quickly that she was startled. His eyes flashed, and she could see that he was controlling his temper only with an effort.

'Come,' she said more gently. 'I am thinking only of you, my dear. You must not take it amiss. Why should you object to making yourself agreeable to Gina? She has improved so much, as you may see for yourself. Why, one might almost believe that she is one of us.'

Giles was about to turn away. He was seized with the urge to tell her to hold her tongue, but he was incapable of speech. His mother caught at his sleeve.

'Listen to me!' she urged. 'Why must you be so foolish? You won't make the least push to improve your fortunes, even when the chance is there for you. Take care, my boy. If I'm not mistaken your friend Newby will be ahead of you.'

Giles looked at her then, and his mother shrank away. At that moment he looked capable of murder. She knew that she had gone too far, but Giles was too much of the gentleman to vent his anger on her.

'Newby is welcome to try his luck,' he said in a colourless tone. With that he walked back to the others.

Chapter Five

The party broke up almost at once, but not before the girls had whispered a request to Gina.

'May Mr Newby call on us?' Elspeth asked. 'He's promised to show us how to waltz. That's if you have no objection…?'

'None whatever! He can teach me too. We must be in the fashion when we go to Brighton.'

Gina issued her invitation without delay, though she did not mention the reason for it. She'd thought it best to use the excuse of a riding expedition.

'We three are used to riding daily,' she explained. 'But Giles has warned me that it isn't wise to go about without an escort in these difficult times. If the gentlemen would be so kind…?' she looked an appeal at Thomas Newby.

'Glad to, ma'am,' he replied promptly. 'We'd be honoured to escort you, wouldn't we, Giles?'

That gentleman bowed in Gina's direction. 'Under other circumstances it would be a pleasure, ma'am, but I have duties here. I've been away for several weeks, and there is much to do.'

His mother glared at him. 'Nonsense!' she said sharply. 'India has a bailiff, and Anthony will be here. You cannot be indispensable to the place, isn't that so?' She looked at Isham for support.

His Lordship nodded. The situation was beginning to intrigue him. 'I think you should oblige the ladies, Giles. After all, they will not wish to ride all day.'

Giles felt trapped. Everyone seemed to have conspired against him. Now he was left with no alternative but to accept the invitation without giving offence. Still he hesitated. His plans to avoid Gina's company were apparently doomed to failure.

'Do come!' she begged in a low voice. 'The riding is a pretext. Mr Newby has promised to teach the girls to waltz, and they are so excited...'

Giles bowed again. 'It will be a pleasure,' he said without conviction.

'Then shall we say tomorrow...perhaps in the afternoon? We promise not to take up too much of your time.' With that she allowed herself and the girls to be ushered to their carriage, but she was lost in thought as they drove home.

She knew Giles all too well. It was clear that he was determined to avoid her company if possible. Was she being cruel? Perhaps, but her resolution did not falter. He still loved her. She was sure of it. Her offer of casual friendship had been deliberate, as was her untroubled manner when she was by his side.

His efforts to avoid her confirmed what she already

knew. He could not trust himself to pretend that he
no longer wanted her. Her attitude had hurt him, but
better to hurt him now than to run the risk of rejection
if she'd thrown herself into his arms.

She sighed at the folly of men and their foolish
pride. Would a woman have thrown away the chance
of happiness because of such stupid scruples?

She thought not, but then, women were so much
more sensible in these matters. Giles felt that his honour
was at stake. He was no fortune-hunter, and unwillingly
she respected him for it, but she loved him so.

The solution to her problem seemed no nearer.
Giles would not offer for her in his present circumstances.

She might appeal to Anthony for advice, but that
would be a mistake. She must not discuss Giles behind his back. If he found out all would be at an end
between them. She alone must solve this problem.
She longed to think of a way to do so.

Her mouth curved in a wry smile. Why had she
fallen in love with such a stiff-necked creature? Her
money was enough for both of them, and she too
owned estates which needed managing. She knew
well enough that she must not mention them. Giles
would regard such a suggestion as charity, but of what
use were possessions if they stood in the way of happiness? She would never make him see it, so for the
present she would take one day at a time.

The following morning brought the promise of rain.
'Will they come, do you suppose?' Elspeth was

standing by the window gazing anxiously at the lowering skies.

'Nothing is more certain,' Gina comforted. 'When gentlemen make arrangements they do not break their word.'

'But if it rains Mrs Rushford won't believe that we intend to ride. Must we ride, Gina? May we not spend the time in learning to waltz?'

'No, my dear. If the day is fine we shall ride, if only for a short distance. Would you have me guilty of lying to Lord and Lady Isham?'

'No, I suppose not, but if that stuffy Mrs Rushford had not been so disapproving we might have just had dancing lessons.'

'There will be time enough for that when we get back. Now, Elspeth, you must go back to your books if you are to have a holiday this afternoon. Cheer up, my love, after nuncheon you may forget your studies for the rest of the day.'

'Good. May I wear my new riding habit?'

'Of course.' Gina hid a smile. She guessed that there would be much primping before the girls were ready to greet their visitors.

She herself had much to do. Summoning her cook, she discussed menus for the week. Then she spent some time upon her household accounts. The sound of distant hammering reminded her that the builders were at work. She rose from her desk and made a quick tour of inspection.

The men greeted her with respect. Gina knew what

she wanted. At first they'd had some reservations about working for a female. From long experience they imagined that she would change her mind a dozen times about the alterations to the house. It had come as a surprise to find that her plans were clear. Gina had given her instructions and from then on she did not interfere.

Even so, they were under no illusions. Always polite and charming, Lady Whitelaw's keen eyes examined every detail. No shoddy workmanship would do for her.

After nuncheon Gina went upstairs to change. Her dark green riding habit fitted her to perfection. It was severely plain, but it emphasised her tiny waist and the swelling curves of her bosom.

She studied it in the cheval glass and was satisfied. She had been wise to eschew the fashionable frogging and tassels which were all the rage this year. She had not the height to carry off such decoration. Nothing detracted from the excellent cut of the garment and the clean lines made her look taller.

She had just picked up her charming little hat and was preparing to go downstairs when Hanson knocked at her door.

'Madam, you have company,' he announced.

'So soon? They are early. I did not expect them yet...' Her heart was already beating faster at the thought of seeing Giles again.

But it wasn't Giles and Thomas Newby who awaited her in the salon. Her colour rose as she encountered the knowing look of her father's brother, Samuel Westcott.

He came towards her with both arms outstretched, but Gina moved swiftly, so that the sofa lay between them. She gave him a stiff bow.

'Uncle, I am surprised to see you here,' she said in a cool tone. 'Father is not with you?'

'No, no, my dear, but I bring a message from him. He asks if you will dine at the new house on Thursday.'

'I shall be glad to.' Her manner was uncompromising.

'Well, now, don't you have a kiss for your old uncle?' He had rounded the corner of the sofa and was moving towards her.

'Uncle, you had best sit down. If you touch me you'll regret it...'

His expression changed. 'Too good for us now, my girl? You always were a spiteful little minx...' Instinctively he rubbed the back of his hand.

Gina glanced down and was pleased to see that it bore a scar. 'I thought you might have learned your lesson,' she said pointedly.

He gave her a malicious look. 'Little cat! There was no call for you to bite me as you did.'

'On the contrary, there was every reason. Did you think me too young to understand your pawing and your stroking?'

He sniggered. 'Just affection for a pretty niece. If you took it amiss, why didn't you tell your father?'

'He wouldn't have believed me. My father is a man

of honour. He would not imagine that his brother could behave so ill…'

'Tush! What was it, after all? A kiss or two, a hug…?'

'You disgust me!' she said clearly. 'I have not forgotten how you were always pulling me on to your knee, and sliding your hand beneath my clothing.'

'You have a dirty mind,' he accused. 'I'd be sorry to think that my own girls should think as you do.'

There was no amusement in Gina's laugh. 'Pray don't think me a fool,' she said shortly. 'Even at fifteen I was aware of your intentions. You made them clear enough on the day that I left Abbot Quincey.'

'Namby-pamby miss,' he mocked. Even so, he could not meet her eyes.

Gina watched with interest as a flood of colour suffused his face. Samuel Westcott had always been an ugly man and the years had not been kind to him. Always inclined to excess flesh, now he was positively gross. Pantaloons and waistcoat strained over an enormous belly, and his neckcloth strove in vain to contain his double chins. A small mouth and heavy-lidded eyes almost disappeared in folds of fat.

Now those eyes gave her a vindictive look. Then he turned his head away.

Gina found that she was trembling. It had taken years to wipe out the memory of that dreadful day when he had trapped her in the store-room of the bakery and tried to rape her. She'd fought him off, biting and scratching as she did so, but it was the final straw. Next time she might not be so lucky. Her answer had been to flee as far away as possible.

Now she was praying that the girls would not appear. She rang the bell, intending to ask Hanson to send them out of the house on some pretext or other, but she was too late. Dressed in their most becoming habits, Mair and Elspeth hurried into the room.

'Are they here? Hanson said…' Mair stopped and bobbed a curtsey. 'Oh, I'm sorry, we did not know that you had company.'

'This is my uncle, Samuel Westcott,' Gina said coldly. 'He is just about to leave…'

Both girls stared at her in astonishment. This was not the gentle, friendly Gina they knew.

Samuel Westcott had struggled to his feet, but now he sank back again on to the sofa. 'I'm in no hurry, Gina,' he said smoothly.

She saw with dismay that his tiny eyes were gleaming as they roved over Mair and Elspeth. 'Charming, quite charming!' he announced. 'Tell me, my dears, when do you make your come out?'

'The girls are too young to think of it as yet,' Gina said sharply. 'I'm afraid you will have to excuse us, Uncle, but we have an appointment…'

'Of course.' He struggled to his feet again, but his eyes were fixed on the girls. 'You'll bring the young ladies with you when you come to dine, I hope?'

Gina felt sick. She turned to the girls. 'I have forgot my crop and my handkerchief,' she lied. 'Will you fetch them for me?'

Obediently they went to do her bidding. Then Gina

swung round on her uncle. 'Lay a finger on either Mair or Elspeth and I will ruin you,' she promised.

'Brave words, little Gina. I think you have forgot. I'm a man of substance now.'

'It won't be enough to save you. I have influential friends. I'll make it my business to see that you lose everything, your home, your business and your reputation.'

'Hoping to sink your teeth into me again?' he sneered.

'Not this time,' she assured him. 'I have more experience now. My next attack will leave you crippled.'

He was given no opportunity to reply. At that moment the door to the salon opened and Giles and Thomas Newby were announced.

Giles was at once aware of the tension in the room. Something had happened to shake Gina out of her composure, but her visitor was about to take his leave. As the door closed behind Samuel Westcott he moved to Gina's side.

'You are very pale,' he observed quietly. 'Has something happened to upset you?'

'It's nothing.' Gina shook her head. She had never told Giles the true reason for her flight from Abbot Quincey. There seemed little point in raking up old memories.

'Gina, this is me, remember? I thought we were to be good friends. If you are worried…?'

She decided that a half-truth was better than nothing. 'Well if you must have it, I find my uncle something of a trial. It was a shock to see him here today.'

With commendable tact, Thomas had been studying a picture at the far end of the room. Now he came towards them.

'The rain holds off,' he said cheerfully. 'We shall yet have our ride.'

With an effort Gina recovered her self-control. 'I've promised that it will be short,' she said. 'The girls cannot wait to learn the waltz.'

Thomas grinned as he looked down at his gleaming Hessians. 'I must crave your indulgence, Lady Whitelaw. I ain't no dancing master at the best of times. In these boots I shall prance round like an elephant.'

Gina was forced to smile. 'It was very good of you to offer to teach us, sir. Perhaps if you just gave us the general idea...?'

'That's all you'll get from Thomas!' Troubled by the look in Gina's eyes, Giles made an effort to lighten the atmosphere.

Gina attempted to follow his example. 'And you, Giles? Shall you prance round like an elephant?'

'Don't believe it, ma'am!' Thomas gave her a solemn look, but his eyes were sparkling. 'Giles is one of those aggravating creatures who can carry a tune in his head, and then transfer it to his feet. He'd make his fortune on the stage, I shouldn't wonder.'

'Very droll, Thomas! Will you be my manager?'

'Glad to, old son! Glad to!' With this promise Thomas turned to greet the girls.

Their ride that day was more of a leisurely ramble. Mair and Elspeth chattered non-stop, quizzing Thomas about his visits to London, and requesting anecdotes about the literary lions and other celebrities.

Giles and Gina had fallen a little way behind the others. 'Mr Newby is very kind,' she observed as she nodded towards the others. 'He has endless patience with the girls.'

'He has a heart of gold,' Giles assured her. 'Don't be fooled by his jokes and his pretence of being afraid of Stubbins. In a tight corner I'd be glad to have him by my side.'

Gina smiled. 'It isn't difficult to penetrate below that light-hearted manner. I like him very much.'

'I'm glad to hear it,' Giles said stiffly. Then he gestured ahead. 'Shall we catch up with them?'

Gina spurred her horse into a trot. She had no need to look at her companion's face. She'd heard the note of jealousy in his voice. She had no doubt that he was fond of Thomas, but having found her again so recently, he was in despair at the thought of losing her to a rival.

For a moment she was tempted to reassure him, but the time was not yet right. Whatever it cost her she must wait. The stakes were too high for her to lose the least advantage. Giles must woo and win her for the second time. She would not make it easy for him.

Was she setting her sights too high? It had been a gamble to come back to Abbot Quincey in the hope of regaining his love. In time she might persuade him to set aside his scruples, but for that to happen he must want her more than anything in the world.

Now an uglier problem troubled her. Would she have returned to the village if she'd known that she and the girls would meet Samuel Westcott? She'd thought herself safe from that creature with his vicious tendencies.

Naturally, she'd made enquiries before leaving Scotland and Anthony had assured her that her uncle was based in London. A successful grain and feed merchant, his visits to his birthplace were said to be infrequent. It was sheer chance which had led him to visit his brother so soon after her return. Hopefully, his stay would be brief.

As they turned for home Giles studied her face again. He was at a loss as to know what to say to her. It was clear that she had no intention of taking him into her confidence, but he longed to comfort her. It was Thomas who broke the silence. He'd been speaking to the girls about their home in Scotland.

'Shall you miss that country?' he asked Gina. 'I hear that it is beautiful.'

'In places it is grand and wild,' she replied, 'but the Whitelaw estates are on the west coast. There we escape the savage winters of the north...'

'Gina says that it is because of the warm Gulf Stream,' Elspeth told him. She was proud to air her knowledge. 'We have grown peaches out of doors...'

'Good farming country?' Thomas was hoping to draw Giles into the conversation.

Gina had recovered her composure. 'We grow an

excellent crop of heather,' she said drily. 'The soil is too poor and thin for us to raise good crops, but our beef is the best in the world.'

'And you should see our Highland cattle, Mr Newby,' Elspeth continued to chatter on. 'They have enormous horns, not like the cows in England.'

'They sound ferocious,' Thomas grinned. 'Did I tell you that I was once chased by a bull?'

'Only because you waved your cloak in front of him.' Giles turned to the others. 'Thomas was inspired by tales of the Spanish matadors. He thought that fighting a bull must be easy.'

'I found out that it wasn't. I must have broken all records to reach the hedge ahead of the beast. I swear I thought he had me. I could feel his breath upon my neck.'

This story was greeted by shouts of laughter, and Gina's good humour was quite restored.

'Giles, you are the expert on good farming methods,' she said quietly. 'I wonder if you would advise me. The Scottish estate is in poor case. My husband, as you know, was never strong. He was unable to oversee the place as he would have wished. Would you think it possible to bring it round? It is a part of the girls inheritance, so it is a matter of some concern to me.'

Giles was interested in spite of his determination to distance himself from Gina.

'I know nothing of conditions in Scotland,' he admitted. 'Mostly what is needed is an injection of capital. One must not throw good money after bad, of course. It's important to decide on the priorities.'

'I understand.' Gina skirted carefully around the question of capital. With the means at her disposal it would not be a problem, but with Giles the mention of money would always be a touchy subject. 'How would I decide on my priorities?'

He gave her a suspicious look. Was she about to offer him some help? That he could not bear.

'Your bailiff will advise you,' he told her abruptly.

'You haven't seen him, Giles. The old man is well on in his seventies, and much opposed to change.'

He smiled then. 'I know the problem. I have the same thing here. Over the years my suggestions have either been agreed to and then ignored, or greeted with dire predictions as to what will happen when one flies in the face of nature.'

'But you *have* made changes, haven't you? Anthony tells me that you have insisted on the use of your new ploughs and seed drills, as well as fertilizers and the correct rotation of crops.'

'You are very well informed,' he said drily.

'I was interested.'

'Really?' Clearly he did not believe her.

'Oh come!' she replied. 'I think that you have forgot that I am country-bred. Anthony lent me a book on Coke of Norfolk. You'll have heard of him, of course?'

'I met him, Gina.' Giles gave up all pretence of indifference. 'The man is a genius. If every farmer could be persuaded to follow his example we could be almost self-sufficient in the matter of food.'

'I can see that that would be important, especially in time of war...'

'It's true. Of course we have the weather to contend with in this country, but there are now new strains of seed which are resistant to both wet ground, and a lack of sunshine, and disease.'

'Is that why you designed your latest seed drill?'

Giles looked his surprise. 'You've heard of that?'

'Of course. Anthony intends to make good use of it. How did you come to invent it?'

'Out of necessity,' he told her briefly. 'The Rushford estate had been run down for years. I couldn't afford to employ much labour. Hand-sowing was out of the question. The drill does the work of several men, but it won't be popular, I fear.'

'You think you may have the same problems as the factory-owners? I mean, won't the local people feel that you are taking the bread out of their mouths, by adding to the unemployment?'

'I couldn't afford to employ them anyway,' he told her. 'With better crops prosperity may return and bread will be cheaper.'

'Prosperity will return in time,' she said warmly. 'Oh, Giles, if only this war were to end... Will Wellington take Badajoz, do you suppose? He is thought to be pushing back the French in Spain.'

'He has done well to date.' Her companion's face grew sombre. 'What a task he had, with his allies fighting among themselves, breaking their promises of men and supplies, and letting him down upon all sides.'

Thomas had ridden on ahead with the girls, but now he came back to them.

'You look as if you are putting the world to rights,' he commented cheerfully. 'Giles, I wonder if we should go into the village before the ladies.' He gestured ahead. 'There seems to be some bustle in the High Street, with people milling about and a lot of shouting.'

'A riot?' Giles asked quickly. 'That's strange…the Luddites operate at night for the most part.'

'I don't know. It don't sound ill-humoured. There's a lot of hallooing and hazzas, and some are waving flags. Still, it might be best to take no chances…'

'Could it be that there is news of a victory?' Without waiting for the others, Gina spurred her horse ahead.

She was right. English tongues had difficulty with pronunciation of the Spanish town of Badajoz, but cheers for Wellington soon convinced her of his victory. She turned to the others with a glowing face.

'Come!' she cried. 'This is a cause for celebration!' She hurried indoors, instructing Hanson to bring up a couple of bottles of her finest burgundy.

As they toasted the Duke's success they shared in the general feeling of elation. Even the girls were allowed a half-glass each, diluted, though it grieved her, with a little water.

Mair twirled about the room, her usual shyness forgotten. 'Oh, I have never felt more like dancing!' she cried. 'Gina, will you play for us?'

Gina laughed. 'A waltz? I don't believe I know a single tune. I've played only for country dancing.'

'It ain't difficult, ma'am. They call it three-four time.' Without the least trace of affectation Thomas began to sing in a pleasant baritone and Gina was quick to follow his lead.

In spite of his claims of clumsiness Thomas was light on his feet and a born teacher. Gina complimented him upon his skill in explaining the steps.

'No trick to it, Lady Whitelaw. I just remember my own difficulties... Now, Giles, if you will take Mair, I shall partner Elspeth.'

Within a half-hour he had them performing very creditably.

'There now,' he assured the girls. 'You'll be more skilled than half the dancers in the room.'

'But what of Gina?' Elspeth protested. 'She has been playing for us and she hasn't had her lesson.'

'Let me play,' said Mair as she moved over to the spinet.

Gina gave up her place with a laughing protest and turned to Thomas Newby. 'I've been watching carefully,' she said. 'I promise not to tread upon your toes.'

Thomas took her in his arms, his hand upon her waist and holding her at a careful distance. In their innocence the girls thought nothing of this close and unusual proximity of their partners, but Gina found it strange.

Thomas smiled at her. 'Relax!' he said. 'You must not hold yourself so stiffly, ma'am. Give yourself to the music.'

Gina tried to obey him, but it was several minutes before she felt at ease. Then suddenly the rhythm became familiar and she almost forgot her partner in the sensation of spinning about the room in a dizzying whirl.

'It feels like flying,' she admitted as the music stopped. 'Mr Newby, you have introduced us to a delightful pastime.'

'Glad you enjoyed it, ma'am, but you must dance with Giles to enjoy it to the full.' He took her hand and led her over to his friend.

This was something that Gina had intended to avoid at all costs, but she could think of no way to refuse. Looking at Giles, she could see that he was equally unwilling, but when Mair began to play he took her in his arms.

Gina felt that her feet were made of lead, and she stumbled over the first few steps, quite unable to follow his lead. She caught her breath. She must not make a fool of herself, but it had been so long, so very long, since he had held her close to his heart.

Everything about him was familiar—the touch of his hand, the faint scent of soap and the outdoors, the power of the arm which encircled her and the knowledge that his lips were a mere few inches from her own.

At length she stole a glance at him, but the handsome face was a mask. It didn't fool her for a moment. To outward appearances Giles was in full control of his emotions, but she was close enough to sense the rapid beating of his heart.

Chapter Six

Gina resumed her seat at the spinet. She would play for the others, but no amount of entreaty could persuade her to dance again.

Thomas remarked on it as he rode back to the Grange with Giles.

'You know Lady Whitelaw better than I,' he said. 'Do you suppose I have offended her?'

'Great heavens, why should you think that?'

'Oh, I don't know. I thought she seemed a little distrait when we arrived today…not quite herself, if you know what I mean.'

'I do, but I can't tell you the reason for it. Perhaps her uncle brought bad news…'

'Possibly. I wondered if she had had second thoughts about my offering to show her the waltz. She did not seem to wish…I mean, she may have found it unpleasant to find herself in the arms of a stranger. I wouldn't upset her for the world.'

'I'm sure that isn't true.' Giles cast a quick look at

his companion. 'Don't allow it to worry you... She
holds you in high regard. She told me so herself.'

Thomas brightened. 'Do you say so? I am glad of
it.' He rode on in silence for several minutes. Then
he returned to the subject.

'There's something I want to ask you,' he said in
a low voice. 'Don't take it amiss, old friend, or think
that I am prying, but have you a *tendre* for the lady?'

Giles stared at him, and Thomas flushed to the
roots of his hair.

'I have a reason for asking,' he explained uncom-
fortably. 'I mean, I would not wish to offer for her if
it should clash with your own intentions towards her.'

'I have no plans to marry,' Giles said in a harsh
tone. 'I thought you felt the same.'

'I did...that is, until I met her. She's everything a
man could wish for. I hadn't thought to meet any
woman with her qualities. She's so full of courage
and intelligence. Surely everyone must love her. That
smile turns a man's knees to water.'

Privately Giles agreed with him, but he was filled
with feelings of despair. Gina might be wealthy, but
Newby's family could match that wealth. Thomas
could not be considered a fortune-hunter. His father
had always made it clear that he wished for nothing
more than to see his son safely settled with a suitable
bride. Handsome settlements would follow.

'This is a quick decision on your part,' Giles said
carefully. 'Are you sure of your feelings for Gina?
You've been in love before, or so you tell me.'

'Mere infatuations!' Thomas dismissed his previous liaisons with a wave of his hand. 'Up to now I had not thought of marriage. Of course, I may not stand a chance with her. She may already have plans in that direction. Do you know if that is so?'

'She hasn't mentioned anyone,' Giles said stiffly. 'Though I doubt if she would discuss such matters with me.'

'But you are her close friend, are you not? You always seem to have so much to say to each other.'

'Our conversation has been mostly about farming practice.' Even as Giles spoke he saw the look of surprise on his companion's face. Truly, it must seem odd to be discussing agriculture with such a warm and loving woman.

'Gina is something of a diplomat,' he continued. 'It's part of the secret of her charm. She is accustomed to speak of others' interests rather than her own.'

'I see. It doesn't surprise me. I think her the most agreeable person in the world. How her face lit up when we heard the news of the victory of Badajoz.'

'Isham will be able to tell us more. He'll have the news by now, I make no doubt.'

Giles was right. When they reached the Grange they found Lord Isham in his study, reading a lengthy missive which had been delivered by special messenger.

'Good news at last!' Isham laid aside the papers. 'Have you heard already?'

'We have…the village is *en fête*. What can you tell us about the engagement? Was the victory complete?'

'It was. There is a darker side, of course. The Duke was delighted by the bravery of his troops, but then they let him down. Serious looting followed, and the men got out of hand. He wasted no time in restoring order. He was forced to resort to floggings and two men were hanged.'

'For looting?' Thomas was incredulous. 'I thought that it was common in time of war.'

'Not in Wellington's army. He has always insisted that goods requisitioned from the Spaniards should be paid for, which is why we are more popular than the French, who leave the populace with nothing.'

'Even so, it does seem hard when the men have fought so well...'

'His Lordship understands his troops. His army is not made up of gentlemen, you know. On occasion he has referred to them as the ''scum of the earth''. On another he mentioned that he hoped that they would terrify the French, because they certainly terrified him.'

'Yet they follow him without question,' Thomas said in wonder. 'Why is that, my lord?'

'He cares about them in his own way. At times he has turfed his officers out of comfortable billets when they've left their men unfed and without shelter. The troops know him as a hard man, but he is just, and he won't waste lives.' Isham looked at his brother-in-law. 'You are very quiet, Giles. Do you disapprove of Wellington's draconian measures?'

'No! I must suppose he had no choice. It must be difficult to control a drunken rabble.'

'It was. Once they found the stores of wine they drank themselves into oblivion, after raping half the womenfolk. That was one reason for the hangings.' He looked up with a smile as India entered the room. 'Come in, my love. We are just discussing this famous victory.'

'It seems to be a day for news,' she told him. 'The servants have heard that there may be trouble at the Abbey. Yardley has been to see the Marquis. He's thought to believe that Sywell may have killed his wife...'

Isham rose from his desk and took his wife in his arms. 'You must not listen to rumour, India. This is gossip, pure and simple. No one can be sure of what has happened.'

'Then you still believe that she has run away? Oh, Anthony, I do so hope so. Another murder would be more than I can bear.'

Thomas was looking mystified, and India was quick to notice it.

'I do apologise,' she said. 'You cannot have heard the story, but the villagers have thought of nothing else for months.'

'Giles told me that the Marchioness was missing,' Thomas admitted. 'Pray, ma'am, don't distress yourself. Sywell has an evil reputation, and his wife, so I understand, is but a girl. Is it not more likely that she found her life with him intolerable, and decided to go away?'

Lord Isham gave him an appreciative look. 'There,

my love, you see that it is obvious. Would you not have run away yourself?'

'I'd never have married him in the first place,' India said with feeling.

'So you married another ogre instead?' Isham's eyes were twinkling.

'A dear ogre!' India squeezed her husband's hand. 'Shall we dine at home tonight?'

'I believe so, my dearest. Then you may regale Mr Newby with the full story of Sywell's iniquities.' Isham smiled as he looked at his companions. 'It is a favourite topic with my wife,' he explained.

'How can I ignore them?' she protested. 'The man has ruined half the village girls. Now they are left to bring up his children. I beg your pardon, Mr Newby. It is an ugly tale and I should not trouble you with the details.'

'But, ma'am, he cannot still be up to his old tricks? His age must tell on him, I feel.'

'That's true, but how I wish that he would sell the Abbey and move elsewhere. I can't imagine how he manages to run the place. The villagers avoid him, except for Aggie Binns, the laundress, who goes in from time to time. Apart from that he has only a single manservant.'

'Solomon Burneck must be a masochist,' Giles announced with feeling.

'You are right. Not only does he put up with his master's rages, but he must find it difficult to persuade any of the local tradesmen to supply the Abbey. A mountain of debt has ruined one or two of them.'

'A thoroughly undesirable character, ma'am. You would be well rid of him.'

'I think so, but he gives no sign of leaving Abbot Quincey.'

Thomas grinned. 'He could be struck by lightening, Lady Isham.'

'That fate would be too good for him,' India said with feeling, but she was laughing as she left the room.

Isham felt relieved, but he summoned his butler without delay.

'You will call the staff together,' he said firmly. 'I want it clearly understood that Lady Isham is not to be troubled by gossip. Anyone who disobeys my orders will take the consequences.' As always, he did not raise his voice. There was no need. Isham did not make idle threats. He turned to his companions. 'Shall you care to fish tomorrow?' he enquired. 'I can promise you good sport.'

Giles was tempted to protest that he had work to do, but his brother-in-law forestalled him.

'It will give you an opportunity to check the work of the water bailiffs, Giles, and Mr Newby will enjoy it, as I shall myself.'

There seemed little more to say, but Giles was longing to lose himself in the more detailed work of checking the accounts. It was all very well to be invited to fish the river, but it would give him time to think of Gina.

He couldn't dismiss her from his mind, and his conversation with Thomas seemed to have tied his stomach in knots. Why should he have been surprised by Thomas's decision to offer for her? He should have suspected something of the kind.

To be fair, he knew that Thomas had not considered Gina's fortune. His friend had seen only a charming woman, little more than a girl, possessed of wit and a delightful sense of humour. Gina was no fool, and that, allied to her vivid little face and voluptuous figure, had been enough to sweep Thomas Newby off his feet.

For Gina it would be an excellent match, Giles thought miserably. He'd already convinced himself that she would marry again, and Thomas was an eligible suitor. He was of good family, his wealth would match her own, and all other considerations aside, Thomas was a kindly, good-humoured person. His wife would come first in all his dealings. Gina could do far worse.

The thought did not comfort him. It was useless to hope that Gina would refuse his friend. Had she not admitted that she liked him very much? It might be a short step from there to feelings of true affection. When Thomas went upstairs to change Giles turned into his tiny office and busied himself with a new design for his seed drill.

After only a few moments he threw his pen aside in disgust. Inspiration would not come, and after all, what was it? Hardly a scheme to cause a woman's heart to beat a little faster. Gina must think him a dull dog, in spite of her pretence of interest in his inventions. In the blackest of moods he summoned his valet and went upstairs to dress for dinner.

Gina, as he had suspected, had much upon her mind. She'd accepted her father's invitation with much pleasure, though, at the time, she hadn't imagined that her uncle planned to extend his stay in Abbot Quincey.

Now she was in a quandary. She was tempted to go alone, claiming that Mair was suffering from a migraine and that Elspeth had stayed behind to keep her company. Would she be believed? Unsure, as yet, of their changing position in society, her parents might imagine that they were unfit to entertain the daughters of Sir Alastair Whitelaw. She could not risk it.

Yet the risks of taking the girls into Samuel Westcott's company might be even greater. She shook her head impatiently. Her warnings to her uncle had been clear. In a family gathering he would not dare to make advances to the girls, and she would watch him like a hawk. Even so, she could not feel easy in her mind.

Two days later, as they set off for the new house, she looked closely at her charges. It had been a struggle, but Mair and Elspeth were now clothed in the most modest of garments. The high necks of their gowns and the long sleeves were perhaps unsuitable for a dinner engagement, as they had told her.

'Bear with me!' she'd said. 'This is quite different from your visit to Lord and Lady Isham. I would not have my parents think that you intended to pull rank.

They are simple people, and they would not take it kindly.'

It was enough to convince the girls that they must do as she wished.

That evening she was proud of them. Their curtsey to her mother and father had been deferential, and their manners could not be faulted. At dinner she was careful to make sure that they were seated by her side, and far from any possible attention from Samuel Westcott.

That gentleman was surrounded by the members of his own family. The older girls were married, as was his eldest son, but George, the youngest, had accompanied his father.

Gina had greeted the young man without enthusiasm, but now she took herself to task. He must not be blamed for his father's misdemeanours. George was quiet and polite, but he was quick to address himself to putting the girls at ease.

Gina looked around the table, marvelling at the fine array of plate and glass. By dint of hard work her father had done well, and now he was proud of his new home.

'Well, Gina, what do you think of it?' he asked proudly.

'I think it very fine,' she said. She turned then to her brother and questioned him about his family. He answered readily enough, but Gina was conscious that his wife's eyes were resting upon her in no kindly way. She had no way of knowing that a bitter conversation had ensued earlier that evening.

'So your father is to kill the fatted calf?' The younger Mrs Westcott had complained. 'I don't see why we are to make a fuss, when Gina ran away without a word of explanation.'

'Hold your tongue!' her husband had replied. 'Gina is now Lady Whitelaw. You will treat her with respect.'

'Oh, hoity-toity! I wonder if your sister will do the same?'

It seemed unlikely. The former Miss Westcott eyed her younger sister with undisguised envy.

'Gina, where do you buy your clothes?' she asked. 'I think you did not purchase that gown in Abbot Quincey.'

'I've had it for some time,' Gina told her quietly. 'If you wish I'll give you the name of the woman who made it for me in London.'

'The famous Madame Félice?' her sister jeered. 'Her prices are above my touch.'

'No, she does not dress me. I am not quite in her style. She looks for those who will carry her creations well. I am too short, you see.'

'But you look charmingly,' George Westcott assured her shyly.

'It is kind of you to say so, sir.' Gina turned her attention to her cousin. 'Are you based in London with your father?'

'No, ma'am. I am here to learn the business from your father. My elder brother will take over the London side...'

'And are you happy in Abbot Quincey?'

'I like it here. London is all dirt and noise and bustle. I prefer the country.'

Gina warmed towards him. His father might be anathema to her, but this young man, though shy, was eager to please. She was happy to encourage him, a fact which did not escape her mother's notice.

When the ladies retired she took Gina aside.

'What do you think of your cousin George?' she asked without preamble.

'I like him. Is he living here with you?'

'He is. George has always been a favourite of mine. Had you not gone away, we hoped that in time you and he would make a match of it.'

'First cousins, Mother? Surely that can't be?'

'There is no law against it, Gina, either from Church or State…'

'But it can't be wise. Interbreeding brings such dangers…'

'Not always. I could tell you of many successful marriages between cousins.'

Gina gave her mother a steady look. 'Don't set your heart on it, I beg of you. I would never consider it.'

'Your uncle Samuel will be disappointed. He thinks it best for the family…'

'For *his* family, perhaps, but not for me. I don't intend to marry again just yet, and when I do the choice will be mine alone.'

'Oh, Gina, you haven't changed! Always a hot-head! It can't be right for you to live alone. Don't you want children of your own?'

'In time, perhaps, but not just yet. I have the girls to think of…'

'Take care that you don't wait too long,' her mother warned. 'Youth does not last for ever.'

Gina smiled. 'I'm not at my last prayers, nor am I in my dotage. Trust me, mother dear, I may surprise you yet.'

'Then there is someone…someone who is dear to you?'

Gina seemed not to have heard her mother's last remark. She turned her attention to the girls, to find that George was entertaining them with stories of ghostly happenings at the Abbey and the sighting of mysterious lights in the woods.

'I don't believe a word of it,' Mair said stoutly.

'I do!' Elspeth gave a delicious shiver.

George heard a grunt of displeasure from his father. He was at a loss to understand it, but perhaps he had been wrong to frighten the girls. He stopped in mid-sentence and addressed himself to his hostess.

'I must thank you for an excellent dinner, Aunt. I much enjoyed it.'

'Aye, lad, and you did it justice.' His uncle beamed at him. 'I like to see a good trencherman.'

Gina smiled to herself. Her father had always prided himself on keeping a good table. 'Father, you'll put me to shame,' she teased. 'I must have the recipe for those mushroom fritters and the curd pudding. You'll dine with me next week, I hope?' By that time she hoped that Samuel Westcott would have returned to London, so she did not include him in the invitation.

'We'll see...we'll see! Your fine friends may not care to meet the likes of us...'

'They'll be delighted, Father, but if you prefer we shall make it a family party. George must come too, of course.'

She knew that her father was pleased with the invitation. Society was changing fast, but he was of the older generation. Wealthy as he was, he prided himself on knowing his place. He had no desire to be thought encroaching. With him it was still a touchy subject and he had no wish to risk a snub from any member of the aristocracy.

'You'd like to see the rest of the house, I expect?'

Gina nodded. Good business management and hard work had provided her parents with the means to build this symbol of their success. She was delighted for them.

'I believe I'll take a turn round the garden,' Samuel Westcott said. 'I fancy a pipe of tobacco. George, what do you say?'

George looked startled. His father did not often evince a desire for his company, and he had never smoked. He left his other cousins to their gossip and followed Samuel on to the terrace.

The reason for this private conversation was not far to seek. Samuel rounded on him with a curse.

'Damn your eyes!' he hissed. 'What are you about, my lad?'

George was mystified. 'What is the matter, Father?

Should I not have spoken of the ghosts and the lights in the woods? I thought the girls did not seem frightened, but perhaps I'm wrong.'

'Perhaps I'm wrong,' his father mimicked. 'I'll tell you how wrong you are! Here is your cousin, Gina, with more money than any woman has a right to own, and you must waste your time in talking rubbish to those girls.'

George stared at him, open-mouthed.

'Perhaps you think to fix your interest with one of the Whitelaw girls? I'd advise you to forget that scheme. I know Gina. Neither of them will be allowed to wed the son of a grain merchant, however wealthy.'

'It hadn't entered my head,' George replied with dignity. 'They are little more than schoolchildren.'

'The elder one comes out next year, but that's beside the point. Gina should be your target. She is one of us. There can be no difficulty there. You and she are of an age and she's a cosy armful. Wed her, and you'll keep the money in the family...'

'Why should she consider me? We hardly know each other.'

'What has that to say to anything? Goddammit, boy, can't you make a push in your own interest? She don't appear to have taken you in dislike.'

George gave his father a mulish look. 'I won't do it,' he announced. 'For one thing I'm already promised...'

'Really?' Samuel Westcott's tone grew silky. 'And who, may I ask, is the object of your affections?'

'Ellie works in my uncle's bakery.' George awaited

an explosion, but when it came he was astonished by the virulence of his father's anger.

Samuel seized his arm, thrusting his face up close. Then he began to curse with great fluency.

'I won't listen to this.' George began to walk away.

'Don't turn your back on me, you dog! Will you throw yourself away on some trollop of a servant girl? I suppose you've got her in the family way?'

'Ellie will become my wife,' his son assured him. 'Her family is respectable, and you shall not malign her.'

'Shall not? Who are you to tell me what I shall and shall not do? Let me tell you this, if you defy me, you won't see a penny of my money.'

'I don't want it,' George said simply.

'But you want your job with your uncle, don't you? I need only tell him that I've changed my mind and I want you back in London. As for this wench of yours, I'll think of some excuse to get her turned off without a reference, and that won't be all she'll suffer.'

'No! She is the only breadwinner in her family…'

'Well then, you won't wish to injure her.' Samuel had not expected such resistance from his normally docile son. He decided to change his tactics. 'Gina will wed again, and we all wish her well, I believe. There is naught to say that you cannot make a friend of her…be agreeable, I mean?'

'Nothing at all,' George agreed. 'I like her very much.'

'Well then, why not spend some time with her?

Gina has been away for years. She knows few people here in Abbot Quincey. It would be a kindness to make yourself useful to her. Won't you please your old father in this at least?'

'I'll be glad to, but on one condition. You must give me your word that you won't attempt to injure Ellie.'

'Why, lad, I don't even know the girl. I spoke in haste, but out of concern for your best interests. You know my temper, George.'

'I do. Will you give me your word?'

'Of course. Let us be friends again.' Samuel took out his handkerchief and wiped away a non-existent tear. 'There is nothing like family, my boy.'

Privately, George could only agree, but he made no comment. There was nothing like family indeed. It was only the desire to keep Gina's money in the Westcott family that had caused his father's outburst.

The confrontation had shaken him, but it was the threat to Ellie that worried him most. He knew Samuel Westcott to be a ruthless man and his promise could be worthless. Somehow he must think of a way to keep his beloved safe until he was in a position to wed her. Well, two could indulge in deception.

'Do you believe that Gina will marry again?' he asked innocently.

'There's nothing more certain.' Samuel grew jovial. 'Wed to a man who was old enough to be her father, and widowed for two years? Why, she's ripe for plucking.'

'I doubt she'll lack for suitors. There's something

about her, father, that is not in the common way. I find her charming.' Fear for Ellie's safety had made George cunning. He must give the impression that he was not indifferent to Gina.

'I'm glad you think so.' Samuel was pleased to hear that there was still some hope of persuading George to woo his cousin. His attempt to ride rough-shod over his younger son had not succeeded. Now he must be more subtle.

'Gina has faults, of course. She has always been outspoken and accustomed to having her own way, but a vigorous husband will put an end to all that. What she needs is a babe each year. That will calm her down.' Samuel knocked out his pipe and waddled back into the salon.

There he sank down upon a sofa, closed his eyes and pretended to be dozing. It didn't escape his notice that George had gone at once to Gina's side and was deep in conversation.

Samuel was satisfied. In time the lad would come to see where his best interests lay. As for this wench…this Ellie? Perhaps now was not the time to remove her from the scene. Let George believe his promises. He could afford to wait.

Chapter Seven

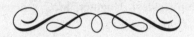

'Gina, I do like gentlemen, don't you?' On the journey home, Elspeth was radiant. She had enjoyed her evening.

Gina laughed. 'Why do you say that?'

'Well, they are all so kind. Mr Newby makes us laugh and Mr George Westcott tells such interesting stories…'

'And can you decide between them? I thought that Mr Newby was your latest flirt.'

'I doubt if I'll ever marry,' Elspeth said artlessly. 'I'll never be able to choose.'

'And does Mair feel the same?' Gina glanced at the elder of her charges.

'I'd need to know them better,' Mair said wisely. 'I feel more comfortable with Giles. He seems to me to have a stronger character.'

'Giles is the handsomest of all, but he doesn't laugh so much…' Elspeth continued to chatter on. 'Still, we love him best, don't you?'

'I hadn't thought of comparing him with anyone,'

Gina replied. It was no more than the truth. Giles alone had touched her heart. Beside him George and Thomas Newby seemed to her to be no more than boys. 'But you have known Giles longer. That is probably the reason.'

Her voice was perfectly steady, but Mair gave her a long look. There was something slightly fey about Sir Alastair's eldest daughter. Mair seemed to pick vibrations from the air.

'Mr Newby has been more than kind,' Gina went on quickly. 'Without him you would not have learned to waltz.'

'And he has promised us more lessons,' Elspeth said with satisfaction. 'Will he come tomorrow, do you suppose?'

'I imagine that he will wait for an invitation, Elspeth.'

'Oh, do ask him again. Promise?'

'We must not monopolise the gentlemen. They will have many other calls upon their time.' Gina was torn between a longing to see Giles again, and the fear that if he took her in his arms once more she would be sure to give herself away.

'But they enjoyed it, Gina. They both said so…'

Gina hesitated. 'Very well,' she said at last. 'You may have your dancing lessons if the gentlemen agree, but I must ask something in return…'

'Anything!' they chorused.

'Anything? Well, I shall take you at your word. If Mrs Guarding has a place for you at the Academy, will you go there willingly?' She studied the stricken expression on both faces with a flicker of amusement. 'It's scarce a sentence of execution, my dears.'

'Oh, Gina, must we? You've always taught us up to now…' Mair was never at ease in a new environment.

'I won't say you must, but it would please me. You would learn much which is far beyond my own capabilities. Besides, you would make new friends. We cannot live in isolation here, and some of the other pupils will be of your own age.'

'It *might* be fun, after all.' Elspeth considered the suggestion. 'We'd hear all the village gossip too…'

'That's hardly a reason for attending a place of learning.' Gina's tone was solemn, but her eyes were twinkling. 'Is it a bargain then?'

'It is,' they both agreed, though Mair looked dubious.

Gina patted her shoulder. 'In your case it won't be long, my love. You'll be out of the schoolroom before you know it and it will be a comfort to have friends about you when you make your come-out.'

Mair smiled, and Gina was satisfied. She tried always to reason with the girls, rather than insisting upon unquestioning obedience. To date, the use of that policy had resulted in the happiest of relationships with her stepdaughters.

'And you won't forget to send a message to the Grange?' said the irrepressible Elspeth.

'I shall pay a morning call on Lord and Lady Isham. We must not continue to deceive them as to the true reason for Mr Newby's visits here.'

'But suppose they disapprove?' Mair said quietly.

'I doubt if they will, my dear, and Anthony is master in his home...'

Gina did not pursue the subject. It was not her intention to criticise Mrs Rushford to her charges. On the following morning she ordered her carriage and set off for the Grange.

She was happy to find that India was receiving, and pleased to realise that she was the only visitor on that particular day.

India greeted her warmly. 'Oh,' she cried. 'How good of you to come! Anthony is out riding with Giles and Mr Newby, and Mama and Letty are gone again to Hammonds in the village. I'd like to have gone with them, but Anthony is concerned about my being jolted in the coach.'

Gina sympathised. 'Perhaps It's better to take no chances in these early days, Lady Isham.'

'Please call me India. We are old friends, are we not? I was feeling sadly neglected, but now I'm glad that I didn't insist on going out, otherwise I should have missed you.' India tossed aside her embroidery with a look of relief. 'Don't look at it!' she pleaded. 'I am no hand with a needle.'

'Nor I.' Gina gave her companion a cheerful smile. 'I think it a total waste of time, though it is considered to be a suitable accomplishment for women.'

'You prefer others, so I hear...' India gave her visitor a curious look.

'Rumour abounds, I know, but I have quite given up the practice of marksmanship and the art of mur-

der.' Even as she spoke Gina recollected the recent
tragedy at the Grange. 'Oh, I beg your pardon,' she
said quickly. 'That was tactless of me.'

When she looked up she found that India was smiling.

'Don't be embarrassed, Gina. I enjoyed your joke.
May I offer you a glass of wine? I must not join you,
but I am allowed lemonade.'

'Then lemonade for me, India. I find it so refresh-
ing.'

Later, glass in hand, she explained the reason for
her visit.

'I have a confession to make to you. I fear it was
a base deceit, but Giles and Mr Newby have been
teaching the girls to waltz.'

'How dreadful!' India said demurely. 'And here we
were, in all innocence, believing that your objective
was to ride. I shall take Giles to task!'

'Oh, please don't!' Gina was betrayed into a quick
objection. 'It wasn't in the least his fault. I allowed
myself to be persuaded by the girls and Mr Newby.
Your brother was against it.'

'Was he? That surprises me. He taught both Letty
and myself, though my mother does not know it.'
India was laughing openly. 'Great heaven, Gina, why
should you think we'd mind?'

'I felt I was deceiving you, but we had no wish to
offend Mrs Rushford's feelings...'

'Mama will learn to move with the times,' India
replied. 'Gina, will you tell me something? You knew
Giles in Italy long ago, didn't you?'

Gina's mouth was dry. She could only nod. Was her secret to be discovered after all this time?

'Forgive me! Perhaps I should not ask, but Letty and I have often wondered why he was so changed when he came home. We hardly knew him.'

'In what way had he changed?' Gina found it difficult to speak.

India frowned. 'He was different in that as a boy he was such a cheerful person. Oh, I don't know how to explain it to you. Letty and he and I were close and he was always the leader in our expeditions, full of energy and ideas. And yet…yet when he returned to Abbot Quincey he was not the same. There was a barrier between us…invisible perhaps, but always there. We did not like to question him, but we have always wondered.'

'You love your brother, dearly, don't you?'

'We do.' A tear sparkled upon India's lashes. 'We'd give anything to have him back to his old self, but we don't know how to help him.'

Gina felt the same, but she did not dare to say so. 'You've already done so much,' she insisted. 'Giles is managing your estate. It is the thing he likes best in the world.'

'It's something,' India admitted. 'But he is so proud. It's fortunate that Anthony is such a diplomat. Giles could not bear to live on charity.'

'But, India, that is not the case. Anthony thinks highly of your brother's expertise, and these inventions must change the face of farming in this country.'

'They might, if they were ever patented. Anthony

has offered to back such a project, but Giles won't hear of it.' India looked at her companion's face. 'Tell me about Italy,' she demanded. 'It was there that something happened to my brother.'

Gina froze. She was silent for so long that India grew alarmed.

'My dear, you are so pale. Do you feel quite well?'

With an effort Gina recovered her composure. 'Forgive me! I have tried for so long to forget those dreadful times…'

'How thoughtless of me, Gina. Pray do not speak of them.'

'Yes, I must. It does not help to keep it all inside one's head. When Napoleon attacked conditions in Italy became chaotic. We were staying in the hills behind Naples. We had to get away, but the children were so young, and their mother suffered from a wasting disease. Sir Alastair himself was never strong…'

She paused then, but when she spoke again her voice was bitter.

'I doubt if you would recognise your fellow human beings, India, if you should see them in the grip of panic. We reached Naples with some difficulty. Several times we almost lost our coach and horses to other refugees. Then, at the harbour, we found that most of the boats were already filled, and by young men. It was the young and strong who were able to save themselves. Women and children and the old were trampled underfoot.'

'Oh, do not tell me that Giles took a place which might have been given to a woman.'

'No, Giles had left the week before. Your uncle sent for him in haste, he tells me.'

'But if all the berths were taken how did you manage to get away?'

'There was a vessel sailing for the Caribbean. I boarded as she docked. Then…er…I held the Master at gunpoint until the family was on board.'

'And you sailed with him? Weren't you afraid of being murdered when you were at sea?'

'Not in the least. I kept my pistols by me at all times, and gold was an added inducement to the fellow, with a promise of more when we reached Jamaica.'

India gasped. 'What an experience! You were little more than a child…'

Gina shrugged. 'One is forced to grow up fast when lives are at stake.'

'And…when you last saw Giles in Italy…did you sense anything amiss with him?'

'No. He came to the villa to bid Sir Alastair farewell before we left for the hills. Your brother was unchanged then.' Gina's heart ached as she recalled that final evening of happiness. She and Giles had promised each other that no obstacle would be allowed to stand in their way. The world was their oyster, Giles had said, and she had believed him.

'We…we had expected to see him on our return,' she continued. 'Sir Alastair relied on him so much, you see, but Giles was nowhere to be found. Then we learned that he had taken ship some days before.'

'Do you know why?' India enquired. She had noticed Gina's quivering lips, and her heart went out to her visitor. With Giles gone, the Whitelaw family must have felt abandoned in a foreign country with anarchy and chaos on all sides.

'My lady…India…you need not explain to me. I believe it was some family matter.'

'It was an emergency,' India told her softly. 'My uncle James sent for Giles in haste. He was needed here on the estate. There was a real danger that it would be lost to us without a strong hand at the helm. I won't go into details, but, believe me, it is true.'

'I never believed that Giles would desert us without good cause. Sir Alastair thought so highly of him, India. Giles did mention that he had sent a note of explanation to await our return to the villa, but we did not receive it…'

'That was unfortunate, but you tell me that events moved fast. Giles must have sailed from Naples before that final exodus turned into a rout.' India was silent for a time. 'Perhaps the change in him is caused by guilt. He would not learn of the horror of those final days until he returned to England. He must have wondered what had happened to you. I'm surprised that he didn't try to seek you out.'

India stole a look at Gina's face. She was aware that when Giles and Gina were together there was a certain tension in the air. Perhaps Gina believed him to be heartless.

Gina seemed to read her mind. 'He did, but we did not return to Scotland for some years. My family had no addresses for me… You must not blame him, India, I do not.'

'You are generous, my dear, but your life has not been easy. Shall you be happy here in Abbot Quincey?'

'I intend to be.' Gina's smile transformed her face. 'The girls have agreed to attend Mrs Guarding's Academy. In fact, I am on my way there now, to see if she has places for them.' Her eyes twinkled as she looked at India. 'You may think me indulgent, but I had to strike a bargain.'

'What was that?'

'More dancing lessons, that is, if your brother and Mr Newby will agree?'

'I'll pass on the message,' India promised. 'I think you may rely on them. When are they to present themselves?'

'Perhaps tomorrow, or the next day? I've warned the girls that we must not monopolise their time…'

'You are doing them a favour,' India laughed. 'By day they are not short of occupation, but of an evening we can offer only cards. I wonder…' she hesitated.

'Yes?'

'What do you say to a charity ball at the Assembly Rooms?'

Gina stared. 'Shall you wish to sponsor such an event? You are still in mourning, I believe.'

'It won't be frowned upon if it is intended to raise funds for those ill-used children in the northern mills.

My aunt Elizabeth is used to arrange these functions, but she is in London for her daughter's Season.'

'It's certainly a worthy cause, and I should be glad to help you, India.'

'I hoped you would. Come tomorrow, and we'll make out an invitation list. Would your mother and father care to attend, do you suppose? Mr Westcott has always been so generous in supporting us...'

'Nothing would give them greater pleasure,' Gina assured her warmly. 'They would be honoured...'

She was thoughtful as her carriage rolled away. Anthony could not have chosen a better wife, nor she a better friend. She'd been tempted to confide in India, but for the moment it was best not to give a full account of what had happened in Italy. She had not lied, but neither had she been entirely frank. She was still preoccupied as her carriage reached the outskirts of Steep Abbot.

Looking about her she decided that it hadn't changed in years. It was still the prettiest, if one of the smallest, of the local villages, set as it was beside the River Steep and surrounded by trees.

A request to see Mrs Guarding gained her entry to that lady's presence. Gina found herself under inspection from a pair of sharp blue eyes.

A brief nod was her only acknowledgement for some time, but Gina's tranquil expression did not change.

'Yes, my lady, what can I do for you?' Mrs Guarding said at last.

'My stepdaughters are in need of education,' Gina explained. 'Lord Isham recommended you.'

'Did he?' There was a slight thaw in Mrs Guarding's tone. 'How old are the girls?'

'Fifteen and sixteen, ma'am.'

'I see, and what have you in mind for them? Deportment, needlework, a little painting and sketching, perhaps?'

Gina knew that she was being needled, and she laughed.

'Nothing of the sort, Mrs Guarding. I want them to learn to use their minds. Philosophy and mathematics, that is what I want for them.'

Mrs Guarding gave Gina her full attention. This young woman's remarks were unexpected. It was time to reverse her initial impression. On the surface Lady Whitelaw appeared to be merely a fashionable hostess—a type of woman she despised. Clearly she was wealthy. Beneath the close-fitting spencer there was a glimpse of a fine silk gown. Mrs Guarding might scorn concessions to the latest mode, but even she could appreciate the skilled hand of a master cutter.

'Where have the girls been educated?' she demanded.

'I've taught them myself.' Gina could have laughed aloud at the expression on Mrs Guarding's face. 'Don't worry, ma'am, they are fluent in French and Italian, and they have some Urdu. Their knowledge of geography and history is good, but their skill with the needle leaves much to be desired.'

Mrs Guarding actually laughed aloud. Then she held out her hand. 'We shall deal together, Lady Whitelaw. Send me your girls. I'll give them some Greek and Latin too.'

'Thank you, ma'am,' Gina said meekly. 'Mair is a studious creature, but her younger sister is…er… irrepressible, I fear.'

'That is no bad thing, Lady Whitelaw. I like a child with spirit. It often denotes an acute intelligence. You need have no fear for them when they are in my care.' Mrs Guarding paused. 'You realise, of course, that I am considered a pernicious influence in these parts?'

Gina didn't attempt to deny it. 'So I've heard,' she said drily. 'You don't allow it to worry you, I think.'

'Certainly not. My teachers and I may be considered radical in our thinking, but we have a strict moral code.'

Gina make no comment.

'I have found it necessary to err on the side of morality. Our notions may be rigid, but how else can we counter accusations that education in a woman leads to immorality and grief?'

'That is nonsense!' Gina said briskly. 'I have no patience with such Gothic notions. Rather, one would suppose that a good education would cause a woman to think before she acted.'

Mrs Guarding smiled again. 'Have you never thought of teaching, Lady Whitelaw? I try to instil these ideas into my girls.'

'I'm honoured, Mrs Guarding, but my teaching has

been confined only to my stepdaughters, and to my-self of course.'

'That is a pity, ma'am. You are a natural teacher, I suspect. Bring your girls tomorrow then, and we shall make them welcome.'

Gina returned to Abbot Quincey well satisfied with the result of her expedition. Mrs Guarding had made no concessions either to her title or her wealth. Her manner was brusque, and her tone uncompromising, but there could be no doubt that she was a woman of sterling character. Poet, novelist, historian? Yes, she was all of these, as Anthony had suggested, but she was also a dedicated emancipationist. Mair and Elspeth could not be in better hands.

They were still unconvinced but on the following day they set out with her on the journey to Steep Abbot, cheered by the promise of a visit from Giles and Thomas Newby either on that day or the next.

Gina was thoughtful as her coachman turned back towards the Isham estate. Time was passing and the month of May was almost upon them. In September, unless she had persuaded Giles to offer for her, she must go to Brighton for a lengthy stay. It left her only this brief summer to overcome his scruples.

Her conversation with India had confirmed what she suspected. Giles still loved her. His affections were unchanged, but he had given up all hope of winning her. The ruin of their plans had tormented him all these years.

He must have suffered agonies of mind when he learned that she had married. Colour flooded her cheeks. Perhaps he believed that wealth and a title were all she cared for. That might account for his distant manner towards her. Sometimes it verged on rudeness.

She straightened her shoulders. He should know her better than that. If he didn't he was unworthy of her love. She was still the same Gina who had given him her arms, her lips, her heart, all those years ago.

On arrival at the Grange she was shown into the salon, with a promise that Lady Isham would not keep her waiting above a moment or two.

She was turning over the pages of the *Ladies' Diary* when the door behind her opened. Gina rose to her feet and turned round with a smile to find that Giles was standing in the doorway.

In that unguarded moment she had the final answer to her doubts. His smile lit up the room as he came towards her with his hands outstretched. Then memory returned and his hands fell to his sides. He gave her a formal bow.

'I beg your pardon, Gina. I was looking for my sister. I did not expect…I mean…'

'India will be down in a short time. I am to help her with her invitations to the charity ball. We thought of the Assembly Rooms…' Gina's heart was beating fast.

Giles managed a faint smile. 'Such a title dignifies the ballroom at the Angel. What does Anthony say to this?'

'Anthony agrees to anything which will please his wife…' Lord Isham strolled into the room. 'Good morning, Gina. I am in your debt, my dear. India will be glad of your help in planning this event.'

'And I am in yours. Mrs Guarding has agreed to take the girls. I saw her yesterday…'

'What did you think of her?'

'I liked her very much.'

Anthony smiled. 'I guessed her to be a woman after your own heart. How did you persuade the girls?'

Gina looked a little guilty. Then she chuckled. 'Bribery, I fear. I had to promise them extra lessons in the waltz…' She glanced up at Giles. 'I hope that you don't mind. Mr Newby was so quick to offer…'

Giles bowed again, but he felt as if a sword had been twisted in his heart. Would this torment never end? Now he must watch his love again as she danced in Newby's arms. To refuse Gina's invitation would have been impossible without giving offence, especially as Anthony would be sure to override any of his claims to be too busy.

'At what time, ma'am?' he asked stiffly. 'Late afternoon, perhaps?'

Gina nodded and thanked him prettily before she was swept away by India into that lady's boudoir.

Isham sank into a chair and stretched out his long legs. 'Swallowed a poker, have you, Giles?' he teased. 'You are mighty formal with an old friend. Poor Gina! She might as well waltz with a broom handle…'

'Anthony…I have neither the time nor the inclination to give dancing lessons…'

'Really?' The heavy-lidded eyes inspected his face.

'Most men would jump at such an opportunity. All else aside, one could not wish for a better friend than Gina.'

'Believe me, I know her worth,' Giles replied in a low voice. 'Everyone must see it, in fact...' he swallowed a lump in his throat. 'In fact, Newby tells me that he intends to offer for her.'

'Does he, indeed? Will she take him, do you think?'

'I don't know!' Giles turned away in frustration. 'He has everything to recommend him, wealth, a noble family... Why should she refuse?'

'She might not care for him enough to wed him.'

'To date that hasn't been her first consideration,' Giles said bitterly. 'She married Whitelaw, didn't she?'

Isham was tempted into a sharp retort, but he held back the scathing words. He would not hit a man when that man was down, and Giles was suffering. That was all too clear.

'I think that you do not know the full circumstances,' he said quietly. 'Whitelaw offered Gina a marriage of convenience. His wife had died, and he was no longer young. He was concerned about the future of his daughters...'

Giles was startled out of his black mood. 'But...but Gina was so young. Why did she agree?'

'Gina is a realist. She has a head upon her shoulders, as well as a kindly heart. She loved the girls, and she was devoted both to Sir Alastair and his wife.' Isham smiled. 'I think I told you I was his supporter at the wedding?'

'Yes, I remember…'

'Until I met Gina I had misgivings. What do they say: "There is no fool like an old fool"? I thought that my friend might have been seduced by the charms of a young girl. I changed my mind when I met Gina. She justified Sir Alastair's faith in her.'

'Then you are telling me that she was never his wife in the true sense?'

'Sir Alastair was old enough to be her father. His girls, he felt, would be charge enough for her, without adding to her burdens by leaving her with children of her own.'

Giles grew thoughtful. 'Perhaps I have been wrong about her. It was a shock to see her back in Abbot Quincey under such different circumstances.'

'She is still the girl she was,' Isham said quietly. He would not pry, but he was pleased to see that Giles now looked more cheerful.

Meantime Gina was resolved that on this evening in particular, she would refuse to dance. The girls should have the young men to themselves, and she would play for them.

This worthy resolution was put to the test when Mair came over to the spinet and offered to take her place.

Gina waved her away, 'Do you carry on, my dear. I turned my ankle earlier today and it is still quite painful.'

Mair gave her a sideways look. 'You haven't mentioned it before.'

'I had no wish to make a fuss…'

Then Giles was beside her. 'Take my arm,' he said firmly. 'It's but a step out to the terrace. Did you not ask for my advice about your grounds?'

Gina took his arm. She made an unconvincing attempt to hobble, but he stopped her.

'Don't worry!' he said quietly. 'I know that you have no wish to dance with me. I don't blame you, Gina. I owe you an apology.'

He cleared his throat, but Gina did not look at him.

'I have misjudged you,' he went on quickly. 'I had imagined… Oh, Gina, I have been so bitter! I deserve to be horsewhipped.'

She heard the anguish in his voice and it destroyed her. Blindly, she reached out a hand to him.

Then suddenly she was in his arms and he was raining kisses on her brow, her cheeks, her eyes. Lifting her face to his, she offered him her lips.

Chapter Eight

For Gina her lover's passionate embrace wiped away all the years of loss and longing, but the mouth which sought her own rested only briefly on her yielding lips.

Then Giles's hands were upon her shoulders holding her away. 'Forgive me!' he said hoarsely. 'I have no right to touch you…no right at all.'

Gina stared at him. She could not have been more shocked if he had struck her.

'Who has a better right?' she asked in amazement. 'Were we not promised to each other? We swore that we would never change…do you remember?'

'I do. Perhaps we have not changed, but our circumstances are different now…' Giles turned and took a few paces away from her. 'I have nothing to offer you, Gina…'

'Have I ever asked for anything? All I ever wanted was your love. I thought you felt the same.'

There was a long silence. 'We were very young…

perhaps too young to understand that love is not enough.'

Gina looked up at his set face. The shock of rejection had left her feeling stunned. 'What else is there?' she asked in wonder. 'We are both free. How many human beings are offered a second chance of happiness?'

'You don't understand. I am dependent upon India and Isham for my employment and even the roof over my head…I could not even offer you a home.'

'I see.' Anger was beginning to overtake despair in Gina's heart. 'You believe yourself to be some kind of a remittance man, living upon the charity of others?'

Giles did not reply.

'Do you claim that you give nothing in return?' she demanded inexorably. 'You must think your brother-in-law a fool. Would he entrust India's estate to an incompetent? I think not. Anthony thinks highly of your skills.'

'That may be true, but it doesn't alter anything. It may be years before I can make my own way in the world…'

Their eyes locked and Gina's hopes plummeted. He would not ask her to wait, and they both knew it.

'You can't think much of my constancy,' she accused.

'I think it is misplaced.' Giles could not trust himself to touch her. 'Sit down, Gina, you must listen to me… You will marry again…and to someone who can offer you what I cannot…'

Gina's anger rose. 'How dare you presume to plan my life for me? I won't have it, Giles.' She left his side and began to pace about the terrace. 'In all these years I never thought you a coward. Apparently, I was mistaken…'

'Perhaps you'd care to explain that statement.' Giles had gone pale. Now his anger matched her own.

'How else shall I describe a man who fears the opinion of the world? What is it that troubles you, the gossip, the sly asides, the envy of those who wished to wed a wealthy widow?'

'You dismiss your fortune lightly, Gina.'

'No, I don't. It's there, and it can't be dismissed, but it is no substitute for love. Oh, my dear, what else can be so important to you?'

'I don't fear gossip, Gina, as you seem to think. The opinion of the world is not of the slightest interest to me. If we were to wed my good sense would be applauded. Is it not the ambition of many men to seek their fortune in a splendid marriage? We see it every day. It is not my way…'

'Then it is just your stiff-necked pride? Perhaps I should take a leaf out of your book. I seem to have abandoned my own…'

Giles heard the bitterness in her voice. 'Don't, I beg of you!' he said gently. 'Let us not strip each other of all dignity…'

When she did not answer he came to stand before her. 'I'm sorry that you think ill of me,' he said. 'I would have it otherwise, but it cannot be…' Then he bowed. 'Shall we return to the others?'

He heard a muffled refusal, and sensing that she was close to breaking point he walked away, leaving her to recover her self-control without the irritation of his presence.

Gina stared across the darkening garden. Suddenly everything about her seemed insubstantial and almost dreamlike. The hurt of rejection had wounded her to the heart and the agony was too deep for tears.

Shaken by the violence of their quarrel, she tried to blot out the memory of those bitter words, but the recollection of her own humiliation could not be erased. She had thrown herself at Giles, begging for his love, only to be refused. It had stung her into unforgivable words of reproach, and now, finally, she knew that her long-held plans had come to nothing.

She was unaware that the music had stopped until Thomas came to find her. Statue-like, she was still gazing into space, oblivious of her surroundings.

'Lady Whitelaw?'

Gina did not answer.

'Lady Whitelaw, is something wrong?' Thomas was all concern. 'You have a headache, perhaps? Is there anything I can do?'

Gina shook her head, unaware that the tears had come at last and were pouring down her cheeks unchecked.

'Oh, my dear…Lady Whitelaw…Gina…pray don't distress yourself. Shall I ask Mair to come to you?'

Wordlessly, Gina shook her head. Then somehow Thomas was beside her, with an arm about her shoulders. He drew her to him, resting her head against his chest.

He didn't question her again, waiting patiently until the storm of tears had spent itself.

'You must think me foolish,' she gasped at last. 'Pray don't mention this to the girls. Where are they, by the way?' She looked about her and was relieved to see that she and Thomas were alone.

'Giles wished to show them his new mare,' Thomas assured her. 'He did not mention that you were… unwell… He said merely that you wished for a little air.'

Gina managed a weak smile. 'He was right, Mr Newby. I found it rather stuffy in the salon…'

'We have been thoughtless, ma'am. We take advantage of your good nature in allowing you to play for us for hours at a time.'

'But I have not played so much this evening,' she protested. 'Besides it is a pleasure…'

'Perhaps so, ma'am, but you must take care not to overtire yourself.' He pulled out a large handkerchief and began to dab at her cheeks. 'You do far too much for others. It is not always wise…'

With her nerves stretched to breaking-point Gina didn't know whether to laugh or cry at his solemn expression. It sat oddly on that normally cheerful face with its snub nose, round cheeks and the dusting of freckles.

'Let me ring for your maid, at least,' he begged. 'We shall none of us think it strange if you should care to retire…'

Gina was almost tempted into a sharp retort. She was longing to tell him not to fuss, but she caught herself in time. She must not allow her own exasperation to cloud the fact that Thomas intended only to be kind. It was just that his solicitude threatened to drive her mad.

What was the matter with her? It seemed that she was never satisfied. Giles had rejected her whilst Thomas had made his adoration clear. Now she longed only for both of them to go away. She needed time and solitude to recover her equilibrium.

Thomas continued to pat her hand, but she drew it quickly from his grasp as the others came to join them.

Elspeth was too excited about the new mare to notice anything amiss. 'Oh, Gina, she is beautiful and Giles has called her Star. He says that she has Arab blood... Will you let me ride her sometimes, Giles? She must go like the wind.'

'She does, but she'd be too strong for you, my dear. She's a skittish creature at the best of times...'

'She did seem nervous,' Elspeth admitted. She glanced up at the sky. 'Do you think she can sense a storm?' Even as she spoke they heard the first rumblings of thunder in the distance. The sky had grown livid, but Gina was glad of the darkening light. It would hide her ravaged face.

She rose to her feet as a flash of lightning lit the garden. Then Thomas urged them to go indoors.

'I'm not surprised that you felt the need of air, Lady Whitelaw. The atmosphere is so oppressive...'

Gina gave him a grateful look. He had given her an excuse for her long absence from the others, and Mair had accepted it, though her eyes still rested anxiously on Gina's face.

Then Giles bowed to her. 'Will you excuse us if we get back to the Grange at once,' he said.

'Of course!' Gina's tone was formal. 'If you hurry, you may escape the worst of what I fear will be a deluge.'

As they took their leave of her, Thomas drew her to one side.

'I'll call on you tomorrow, if I may, ma'am.'

Gina managed a faint smile. 'You are always welcome, Mr Newby.'

'I'm glad to hear it.' His face lit up, but he was blushing. 'I shall want to know how you go on, Lady Whitelaw...' For once his easy manner had deserted him, and Giles was aware of it.

On the journey home he asked no questions, dreading what he might hear. Had Thomas seized the opportunity to offer for Gina? They had been alone in the garden for some time. He stole a sideways glance at his friend, but Thomas was preoccupied.

A moment's reflection convinced him that Gina could not have accepted his companion. Thomas would have been unable to contain his joy. Perhaps he had changed his mind.

At length the suspense was too much for him to bear.

'You are very quiet,' he observed. 'Is something wrong?'

Thomas gave him a shy smile. 'Far from it, old son. I've made up my mind, you know. I asked Gina if I might call on her tomorrow. I intend to ask her to be my wife.'

Giles felt that it behoved him to say something...anything...but the words would not come.

'Now *you* are quiet, Giles. Do you disapprove?'

'How could I? We agreed, did we not, that Gina would be sure to marry again? You have so much to offer her.'

'Then you'll wish me luck? I ain't much of a catch, I fear. Gina could do much better, but I think she likes me, and I would look after her.'

'I'm sure of it.' Giles turned his face away, feeling that his expression must be ghastly.

'The dear little creature needs someone to protect her. It ain't much of a life for any woman on her own, and she has the girls to think about.'

His companion muttered something unintelligible, but Thomas was lost in rapture and didn't appear to hear it.

'I expect you think that we haven't known each other long,' Thomas continued. 'But I fell in love with her on that first day when she threatened me with her pistol.' He began to chuckle. 'I don't believe there is another woman in the world with half her character. Don't you agree?'

Giles could only nod.

'I knew it,' Thomas said with conviction. 'You and your family think so highly of her. Believe me, I shall do my best to make her happy if only she will accept me. You need have no worries for her future.'

Giles could listen to no more. Seizing upon the fact that the storm had broken at last and the rain was now pelting down, he spurred his horse into a gallop and raced towards the Grange.

Sleep eluded him that night. Each word of his quarrel with Gina was etched indelibly upon his mind. What must she think of him? She had offered him her love and he had spurned her. The old adage came back to him. What was it they said? 'Hell hath no fury like a woman scorned.' What would she do now?

He was under no illusions. He had killed the flame of love which had burned so brightly in her heart for the long years of their separation.

She had accused him of insufferable pride, but Gina too was proud. She would never forgive him.

Sheer agony of mind kept him tossing upon his bed for hours. What had happened to his resolve never to be alone with her? That had been a fatal mistake. The urge to take her in his arms was uncontrollable.

Ah, but it had been heaven to hold her to his heart again and to seek those yielding lips. But he cursed his own folly. He had succeeded only in hurting her. Whatever he was suffering now, he deserved it. All the torments of hell would not be enough to wipe out the memory of her bitter words. They were burned into his brain.

Had he known it, Gina herself was regretting those words. She would have given anything to unsay them but it was too late. For her too, sleep was out of the question. She paced her room for hours, writhing under the lash of humiliation and self-reproach.

What had happened to the iron self-control on which she prided herself? Love, it seemed, was no respecter of such attributes. As she reached out to Giles she had forgotten all her good resolutions. Heaven knows, she had waited for long enough before seeking out her love again. She could go on waiting, but he had not asked it of her.

So she had struck out at him in despair, calling him a coward, a weakling who could not face the cynical amusement of their world, and accused him of putting his own pride before their happiness.

In her own heart she knew that she was wrong. Honour mattered to Giles above all else. It was one of the reasons why she loved him so. Honour had caused him to promise her marriage all those years ago, though he was heir to the Rushford estate and she merely a servant. Honour had brought him back to England to do his duty by his family, though it must have cost him dear.

Now it was that same honour which prevented him from offering for her. Giles would accept nothing which he had not earned. For him it was a matter of principle. He could not bring himself to live upon his wife's fortune.

She couldn't bemoan the accidents of fate which had left her in her present circumstances. What was money, after all? To Gina it was merely a useful tool, certainly not to be despised as it eased one's path in life. Yet it could buy neither health nor happiness.

Yet for Giles it was an insuperable obstacle, and she could think of no way to persuade him to change his mind.

After a while she grew calmer. She would not be defeated. Had she not been certain of his love she might have given up the struggle, but the memory of his kiss, brief though it was, set her senses aflame. His response had been as fierce as her own.

She pushed the thought of their quarrel from her mind. What was done was done. There was no point in vain regrets. The mistake had been her own. She had intended to keep him guessing for a time, in the hope that he would try to win back her love. Now he was sure of it. She had given herself away, but she treasured the recollection of that moment when she was held once more against his heart. Surely a love like theirs could not be denied for ever. She would think of some way to overcome his scruples.

Perhaps she should have made him a business proposition in the first place. Inventions such as the new seed drill might be patented. Gina herself knew nothing of such matters, but Isham thought them useful and intended to put them into service on his own estates.

Then she remembered. Isham had already suggested such a scheme to Giles, but his brother-in-law had turned it down. Pride again, Gina thought sadly. Giles was only too aware of Isham's generosity. Had it not been for India's splendid marriage, his mother and his sisters would be living in a tiny cottage on the outskirts of Abbot Quincey dependent upon the goodwill of his uncle, Sir James Perceval.

He himself would be penniless, unable to provide for them. Those months when he had scoured the country looking for employment had left deep scars upon his soul.

Gina's heart went out to him. It would take time to heal those scars. Perhaps as he took control of India's estate and brought it into profit, Giles would recover some of his self-esteem. Honour, she realised suddenly, was all he had left at present.

At last she fell into an uneasy sleep, but she was heavy-eyed next morning. When the girls had left for the Academy she started upon her daily tasks, but she found it difficult to give them her full attention.

Did it really matter, she thought wearily, whether they dined on a green goose or a serpent of mutton that evening. Her gaze was abstracted as cook suggested various side dishes such as mushroom fritters, crimped cod, or boiled tongue with turnips. Then there were decisions to be made as to the various merits of an orange soufflé, a Celerata cream, or a basket of pastries.

Gina forced a smile. 'You will have us twice the size we are,' she warned. 'Let us have something light such as a dressed fowl. We might start with white almond soup with asparagus tips. That is a favourite with the girls, and so is your excellent orange soufflé.'

'That won't keep body and soul together, my lady.' Cook was never slow to protest when she was robbed of the chance to show her skills.

'It will be sufficient for this evening. We have no gentlemen to feed today. When we have dinner guests you shall choose the menu yourself.'

Cook was startled. It was unlike her young mistress not to take the keenest interest in every detail of the management of her household. She said as much to Mr Hanson.

'Madam may have her mind on other matters,' her confidante replied in lofty tones. 'Food, Mrs Long, cannot always be her first consideration.'

'Without it we should none of us get far,' came the tart reply. 'If you consider it so unimportant perhaps I should forget the dish of neats' tongues which I had in mind to make for your supper, Mr Hanson.'

The butler hastened to soothe her wounded feelings with the assurance that her culinary skills were matchless. Neats' tongues were, after all, a favourite with him. He went on to point out that it was largely due to the excellence of her cooking that the Whitelaw family was so healthy. None of the ladies suffered from the headaches or the fainting spells so common among the gentry.

'That's as maybe!' Cook replied. She allowed herself to be mollified by his compliments. 'But Madam ain't herself. Mark my words, she has something on her mind.'

Hanson decided to see for himself. Cook was not a fanciful woman, and she knew her mistress well. If Madam was worried he would do his best to lift the burden from her shoulders.

He tapped gently at the door to Gina's study, and entered to find her gazing into space.

'Shall you wish to see the builder in your usual way, my lady?' he enquired. He had to repeat the question before she became aware of his presence.

'What?'

'The builder, ma'am. Must he give you a progress report?'

Gina stared at him before she replied, almost as if she did not understand the question. Then she pulled herself together.

'No, it won't be necessary. I saw him yesterday and the work is going on well.' She fell silent again.

'Will there be anything else, ma'am,' he pressed. 'Have you orders for me?' Hanson was appalled by his own temerity. In the ordinary way her ladyship was quick to let him know how he could best serve her. It was not up to him to take the initiative, but he persisted.

'Shall you care to ride this morning, my lady?' he asked. 'I could send an order to the stables...' Obviously his mistress was suffering from an attack of the megrims. This happened only rarely, but when it did a long gallop usually restored her to the best of spirits.

'No...! Yes...! I don't know... Tell the groom, I will send word within the hour.'

'Well, Mr Hanson, was I right?' Cook looked at him in triumph.

'I fear you were. Madam is not herself. Let us hope

that she will ride out this morning. For her it is a sovereign remedy for a sad mood.'

Gina was in agreement with him, but there were other claims upon her time. Both she and the girls required replenishments to their wardrobes. Clothing that had been suitable in Scotland would not serve in the softer, warmer climate of Northamptonshire, especially during the summer months. That was, of course, if they were to see the sun at all this year. The last two summers had been disastrous, or so she'd heard.

Idly, she leafed through the pages of *Ackermann's Repository*. India had given her the name of a clever mantua-maker in Northampton, a French refugee, she thought. Even so, she would choose styles, colours and fabrics before she approached the woman.

Gina knew what suited her, and elegance was her aim. She lacked the height to carry off extremes of fashion, such as the famous 'Marie' sleeve which was puffed and ruched with epaulettes, puffed oversleeves and frilled cuffs. In that, she told herself, she would resemble nothing so much as a gaily-coloured mushroom.

Perhaps a plain blue walking-dress in French cambric? And a morning-dress of jaconet muslin, made up to the throat, with sleeves buttoned tightly at the wrists?

She laid the magazine aside, unable to raise even a transitory interest in the coloured plates. She would return to the task later. It would not take her long to decide on the number of round robes she and the girls would require. They could be made in silk or muslin in simple styles and pastel colours.

Evening wear was even less of a problem at the moment. High fashion would be out of place in the country, even when dining with Lord and Lady Isham.

She caught her breath at the thought of returning to the Grange. How could she face Giles again?

For a long desperate moment she was tempted to close the Mansion House and leave for Scotland with the girls. Then common-sense returned. There was nothing to be gained by running away, and much to lose. The girls were settled at the Academy, and Mair, in particular, must be closer to London to make her come-out during the following year.

To flee would be the action of a coward, and cowardice Gina despised above all else. Giles, she knew, would never follow her to Scotland, so she would stay in Abbot Quincey, facing up to whatever the fates might have in store for her.

For the first time the suspicion of a smile touched her lips. Gina was no believer in fate. She had always favoured giving it a strong push. Nor did she sympathise with those who bemoaned a lack of opportunity. Napoleon Bonaparte might be considered a monster by most of her acquaintances, but one of his precepts had stuck in her mind. 'Opportunities?' he had remarked. 'I *make* opportunities.' Gina was fully in agreement with his words.

Well, now she was to be given the chance to put his advice to the test. She rang the bell and ordered her horse saddled and brought round. Her mind was always clearer on a long ride, and the fresh air would do her good.

She was about to go to her room and change from her pale green sacque into riding dress when Hanson reappeared.

'Madam, you have a visitor,' he announced.

Gina frowned. 'I am not receiving this morning, Hanson. You must deny me.'

'Madam, I tried, but the gentleman says that he is expected. It is Mr Thomas Newby.'

'Oh, Lord, I had forgot!' Gina struck her forehead. 'You had best show him in...'

'And your horse, ma'am?'

'I shall still require Beau to be saddled. Mr Newby will not stay long.'

Gina summoned up a smile to greet her visitor. She had not forgotten his kindness on the previous day.

He came towards her looking anxious.

'Have I been importunate, Lady Whitelaw? Your butler said that you were not receiving, and I feared that you were suffering from some malaise. I wished to assure myself that it was not so.'

'Mr Newby, you are very kind, but as you see I am quite well. I gave orders that I was not to be disturbed as I had some matters to attend...' Gina indicated the pile of papers on her desk. 'And then, you know, I am not yet dressed for receiving.' She glanced down at her simple dress.

'You always look beautiful to me,' Thomas said earnestly. 'But I am sorry to have broken in upon your morning's work. Do you find it onerous, ma'am?'

'Why no! I like to keep myself occupied...' Unreasonably Gina was irritated by the note of sympathy in his voice. 'And I am accustomed to dealing with my own affairs...I have done it for so long, you see.'

Thomas shook his head. 'You are so brave, but it must be a strain on you. Ladies have no head for figures, so I understand. Sometimes you must feel the need for help...for a guiding hand perhaps?'

He did not see the flash of anger in her eyes. Gina did not welcome interference, and the only guiding hand which she would tolerate was denied to her. She was almost tempted into a sharp retort, but she bit back the words. Thomas was on dangerous ground, but he meant only to be kind.

'I find that I have a head for figures,' she said mildly. 'Mr Newby, it is good of you to be concerned, but you must not worry about me...'

The next moment Thomas was on his knees beside her chair, endeavouring to seize her hands.

'How can I help it?' he cried. 'Oh, Lady Whitelaw...Gina...I love you with all my heart. I long for nothing more than to share your burdens...to make you happy. That would be my purpose for the rest of my days. Will you marry me?'

Gina was startled into silence. She looked down at the eager face of her companion in shocked surprise, and there was no encouragement in her expression.

'Mr Newby, please get up,' she said at last. 'I am touched by your concern for me, but I fear that it has carried you away. Believe me, I have no thought of marriage at this present time.'

Thomas stayed where he was. 'Tell me at least that I may hope,' he pleaded. 'I'll wait for you for ever, if need be. I mean…until you have given some thought to my proposal. I may not be the cleverest of men, but I can offer you a loving heart.'

'I know that, Mr Newby.' Gently Gina withdrew her hands from his clasp. 'Your heart will be given, in time, to a lady who returns your regard.'

Thomas could not mistake her tone. He rose to his feet. 'As you do not, Lady Whitelaw?'

'I value you as a dear friend,' she said, 'Friendship is important in a marriage, naturally, but there must be something more…'

'You speak of love? But surely that might come in time. I'd do my best to make you love me…'

'Love cannot be forced,' she told him quietly. 'Mr Newby, I have had experience. My late husband was the best of men. He was my closest friend. I have not spoken of this before to anyone, but I want to make you understand. Sir Alastair and I were happy together, but there was something missing… If I were to marry again it would not be on the basis of friendship alone.'

'There are worse things,' he protested.

'True, but there are also better things…' Gina fell silent.

'Is there someone else?' he demanded miserably.

Gina gave him a long look and he blushed to the roots of his hair.

'I beg your pardon,' he said quickly. 'I had no right to ask that question. Will you forgive me?'

'Of course.' Gina smiled at him and held out her hand. 'I intend to ride this morning. Will you go with me, Mr Newby?'

'A pleasure and an honour, ma'am.'

'Then give me a few moments to change my dress. I shall not keep you waiting long.'

She was as good as her word, but they had scarcely left the outskirts of the village before they saw a horseman in the distance, riding towards them at breakneck speed.

'Ain't that Giles? What the devil…? Oh, I beg your pardon, Lady Whitelaw. Didn't mean to swear, but he'll kill both himself and the mare if he don't slow down.'

Giles was upon them before she could reply.

'Turn back!' he ordered sharply. 'I have bad news!' He had eyes only for Gina, and she searched his face in terror. Her first thought was for the girls.

'Mair and Elspeth?' she said faintly. 'Has something happened to them?'

His hand went out to grip her shoulder. 'Nothing like that, Gina, but my news is serious. Spencer Perceval was assassinated yesterday in the House of Commons…'

'The Prime Minister?' Thomas was incredulous. 'Is it a conspiracy?'

'We don't know yet, but we can't discuss it here. When we get back to Abbot Quincey I'll tell you all I know.'

Chapter Nine

Obediently, Gina turned for home. Then Thomas seized her reins.

'Please don't do that,' she said through gritted teeth. 'I can manage Beau myself…'

'But, ma'am, the shock!'

'Mr Newby, I have suffered shock before…' Gina spurred her horse ahead before she uttered words which she would be certain to regret.

Startled by the vehemence of her outburst, Thomas did not attempt to catch up with her. Instead he looked at Giles.

'Never try that again.' Giles shook his head. 'Gina prides herself on her horsemanship. You are lucky she didn't strike you with her crop.'

'Clearly she is overwrought by your news,' Thomas assured him stoutly. 'I'm surprised that she didn't faint upon the spot.'

'Gina?' Giles looked at him in wonder. 'You have much to learn about her, Thomas.'

'I know it,' his friend said sadly. 'I have just this morning offered for her, but she turned me down.'

Giles was seized with an overwhelming feeling of relief. He was ashamed of the sense of exultation which possessed him, and he did his best to conceal it.

'Did she give a reason?' he asked in a casual tone.

'She says that she don't wish to marry again…at least until…until she can give her love.'

He looked so downcast that Giles was moved to pity.

'Don't take it to heart,' he urged. 'Gina has much upon her mind at present, and this latest news must worry all of us.'

'She didn't know of it when she refused me,' Thomas mourned.

'Nevertheless, it is a shocking thing. Perceval was shot in the lobby of the House, with all his friends about him.'

Thomas paled beneath his freckles. 'Will it mean revolution, Giles? I've heard of the French ideas spreading over here. It's barely twenty years since they took to wholesale massacre…'

'Isham doubts it, but he can't be sure. He left for London within the hour to find out what he can. Meantime, I'm enjoined to take good care of the ladies. Shall you wish to return to your home? Your father may be worried.'

'Wouldn't think of it. I have two brothers. They'll take care of my father, if care is needed, but he's a tough old bird, and more than a match for any mob.

He won't take kindly to the thought of a guillotine being set up in the market place of a Yorkshire village.'

'It happened in France,' Giles warned. 'I'm determined to take no chances with our womenfolk.'

'Of course not. I'd be honoured if you will allow me to share the responsibility. Above all, we must not frighten them.'

Giles grimaced. 'My mother is already in strong hysterics. Both India and Letty are likely to have a trying time with her.'

'At least they will comfort each other. Dear little Gina is alone.'

'I think you have forgot her family,' Giles replied with some asperity. 'They live here in the village.'

'Yes, yes! I expect that she will turn to them for protection.'

Much to his surprise, Gina showed no sign of needing protection of any kind. Once inside the Mansion House she drew off her riding gloves and rang for wine before she questioned Giles.

'Can you tell us more?' she asked. 'Was the assassin taken?'

'He was. His name is Bellingham. He is to be tried without delay.'

'Has he confessed his reason for the crime?'

'He has said nothing.'

'That's strange!' Gina mused. 'A fanatic... someone with a cause will usually shout his beliefs to the world at large.'

Thomas stared at her. Instead of indulging in a fit

of the vapours Gina was discussing the murder as a problem to be solved by cool analysis of the facts. Gradually it was being borne in upon him that he didn't know her at all.

She continued in the same vein. 'Do you suppose that he is quite sane?' she asked. 'This may simply be the act of a single madman.'

Giles smiled at her. 'You might be quoting Isham,' he informed her. 'He said as much before he left. Even so, he feels that we should take no chances.'

'Madmen and fanatics?' Thomas was nonplussed. 'Lady Whitelaw, you cannot mean that you have experience with such creatures?'

'Alas, more frequently than I care to recall, Mr Newby. The Indian continent is a hotbed of fanaticism.'

'Oh, my dear ma'am, how very dreadful for you!'

'It was instructive,' she said drily. Then she turned to Giles. 'What would you have me do?'

'For the present you should not ride out too far into the country, and certainly not without an escort. It would be all too easy for some hothead to conceal himself and take a shot at you or the girls.'

He saw the mutinous look about her mouth. He smiled at her again and Gina's heart turned over. That smile, so rarely seen these days, transformed his face, lighting up the room.

'This is not an order, you prickly creature. It's merely a suggestion. Come now, Gina, give me your word! If you won't consider your own safety, I know that you will think about the girls.'

At his coaxing words, Gina's objections vanished.

'You are right,' she admitted in a contrite tone. 'It would be foolish not to take precautions. May I come to visit your sisters this afternoon? India must be worried about her husband's safety in the capital.'

'You'll bring at least one groom?'

'I'll bring two if it will please you.' Unthinking, she held out both her hands to him. 'Am I forgiven for my stubborn ways?'

'Always, my love!' The endearment slipped out before he was aware of it, but Giles did not pay it attention. He continued to hold her hands as he looked deep into her eyes. Neither of them noticed that Thomas had left the room.

'Take care!' Giles whispered. 'Remember, you have given me your word!' He raised her hand to his lips and kissed it briefly. Then he hurried away.

It was not until they had almost reached the Grange that Thomas challenged him.

'You should have told me,' he reproached.

'I've told you all I know.' Giles misunderstood him. 'I didn't hear about the assassination until two hours ago.'

'I'm not referring to that,' Thomas said stiffly. 'I mean...well...had you mentioned that you and Gina...Lady Whitelaw...had a *tendre* for each other I should not have offered for her.'

Giles slowed the mare down to a walking pace. He had never discussed his love for Gina with another soul, but he was not proof against the air of dejection so evident in his friend.

'We knew each other long ago,' he admitted. 'It is ten years since we met in Italy. Gina was little more than a child, and I was a lovesick boy.'

Thomas shook his head. 'She loves you still. I cannot be mistaken. She does not look at me as she looks at you.'

'She is still clinging to a girlish dream.' His friend's tone grew harsh. 'Those can be the most difficult to give up.'

'She is a woman grown.' Thomas was angry. 'Since you met she has been married and widowed, and still she loves only you. Can you dismiss her constancy so lightly?'

'I must. I have naught to offer her.'

'But you will not tell me that you don't return her affection, Giles? I should not believe you. No one can fail to love her.'

Giles gave a muffled groan. 'I need no convincing of that...' He urged his horse into a gallop until they reached the Grange.

Gina herself was feeling much more cheerful. At the first sign of danger, real or imagined, Giles had hastened to her side, clearly concerned about her safety. And he had forgotten his firm resolve to keep her at a distance.

Now she treasured the memory of his smile, his touch and those unnoticed words of endearment which had slipped out unawares.

She ordered a light nuncheon of cold meats and fruit and ate it with much enjoyment.

Dreamily, she held her hand against her cheek, reliving the memory of his kiss. Her lover's defences had crumbled at the first hint of danger to her. She'd been wrong to give way to despair. All was not yet lost.

Then she took herself to task. The danger which she half welcomed had been born of tragedy. She had been thinking only of herself whilst India must be mad with worry about her husband. Isham would take his seat in the House of Lords, just a stone's throw from where the murder had been committed.

Mindful of Giles's warning, Gina ordered her carriage. By now the news of the assassination had spread throughout the village and she could hear isolated bursts of cheering.

Quickly she called her household together to explain that they were in no immediate danger.

Cook was unconvinced. She jerked her head towards the windows. 'Just listen to 'em, ma'am! They are celebrating the poor man's murder, if you please...'

'Idlers and malcontents!' Gina said firmly. 'They are the ones who run away whenever they are faced down.'

'That's as maybe, my lady. I ain't stirring beyond these walls until the troops arrive.'

'Have I asked you to do so?' Gina's cool gaze reduced the woman to silence. Then she turned to her outdoor staff. 'You will carry weapons at all times,' she ordered. 'Neame and Fletcher will accompany me to the Grange this afternoon, and Thomson will drive.'

'Oh, ma'am, you're never going out?' Cook was abashed by her own temerity, but she was fond of her young mistress.

'Indeed I am, but you need have no fears for me. I am well armed myself...'

Cook screamed and threw her apron over her head. 'You'll be murdered, ma'am, I know it!'

'Not if I can help it!' Gina swept out of the room, leaving the weeping woman to be sharply reprimanded by Hanson for letting down the household staff.

''Tis all very well for you,' Cook moaned. 'I ain't been to these outlandish places with the mistress...'

'If you had you would have no fears for her.' Hanson was unsympathetic. 'Now pull yourself together, woman. Will you add to Madam's worries?'

His rebuke was unnecessary. Having made her wishes known to her staff, Gina didn't give Mrs Long another thought. She regarded hysterics as an unwarranted indulgence on the part of any woman.

She changed out of her riding habit and into a high-necked gown of French muslin in her favourite blue. Over it, for warmth, she wore a waist-length jacket with a high collar and long sleeves in a deeper shade of blue. Not for the first time she blessed the introduction of this useful garment, known as a spencer. Then she selected a high-crowned hat in satin straw, trimmed with matching ribbons. It would crush her hair-style out of recognition, but that was not of the slightest moment. She hurried down the staircase, followed by her maid, who was still cramming various small items into a reticule.

'Don't fuss, Betsy!' Gina almost snatched the small bag from her. 'A handkerchief is all I need.'

Without more ado she jumped into her carriage and pulled the check-string.

The journey to the Grange passed without incident, but on arrival Gina was at once aware of the tension in the household.

Letty drew her to one side. 'Mama has upset India,' she whispered. 'She has her in widow's weeds already.'

'Send for the doctor,' Gina advised. 'Perhaps he'd give your mother a sedative.'

'He's on his way,' Letty told her. 'I was worried about India…'

'There is not the slightest need.' India had entered the room. 'I am not so easily overset…except… except that, of course I am worried about Anthony…' Her voice was quite under control.

Gina sat beside her and took her hand. 'Your husband is one of the most sensible men I know. He always looks ahead, my dear India, and on this occasion he is forewarned of possible trouble.'

India's eyes were bright with tears. 'He is my life,' she whispered. 'I could not live without him.'

'And you will not do so. Giles tells me that Anthony believes this crime to be a single act of murder, for what reason we may never know. I suspect the same myself.'

'Then you do not think it the start of an insurrection? Luddites, for example?'

'I doubt it. The frame-breakers have a genuine grievance, as Anthony will have told you, but they are merely trying to protect their livelihood, although it may not be in ways that we commend.'

'But he said...he said that others have infiltrated their movement for purposes of sedition.'

'That may be so, but I have the utmost faith in my fellow-countrymen. They have a strong objection to being used.'

'Oh, how sensible you are!' India smiled through her tears. 'You must think me a veritable watering-pot.'

'I don't think that at all!' Gina pressed her friend's hand. 'All I ask is that you don't meet trouble ahead of time. I've done it so often in the past. Then I've discovered that my worries have been unfounded. In the meantime, I've wasted many unhappy hours in allowing my imagination to dwell upon disaster. Time enough for that if it should happen, and for most of the time it doesn't. Anthony will be back with you before you know it.'

'He said at least a week...' India ventured.

'Quite possibly. I won't make light of this tragedy. The Government must be in disarray, but they will value Anthony's advice.'

India recovered some of her self-possession. 'I expect so. He has been concerned. Oh, I know that he discounts the idea of revolution in this country, but he's aware of the disaffection in the north.'

Gina nodded. She too had heard of the increase in the rioting.

'And then, you know, there is all the unemployment due to Napoleon's blockade. Cotton cannot get through to the towns in Lancashire, and the price of bread is rising constantly.'

'The war will not last for ever,' Gina comforted. 'Wellington is pushing back the French in Spain. When peace comes we shall enjoy prosperity.'

'That may be years away,' India told her sadly. 'Meantime this country is a tinder-box. It needs only a spark to set it aflame.'

'With respect, I think you are mistaken,' Gina replied. 'Take the Prince Regent, for example. He is despised for his extravagance, his bigamy, his mistresses and his treatment of his father and his wife. When he appears in public, he is jeered at and pelted with mud, yet no one attempts to do him serious harm.'

'He is regarded as a buffoon.' Giles had entered the room.

'Oh, no, he isn't that!' India shook her head. 'What the British can't forgive is that he is a patron of the arts. Had he confined his interests to horse-racing and boxing he would have been much more popular.'

'You are very hard on us, Lady Isham.' Thomas smiled down at her. 'Are we then a race of Philistines?'

'I fear you are, Mr Newby. The Prince is suspect because of his passion for orientalism, for design, for luxury, and for exotic foods... These things are not dear to the hearts of people in this country.'

'Especially the latter,' Giles broke in. 'I'm told that the Regent is now so fat that a hoist of some kind is needed to seat him upon his horse.'

Everyone smiled, but Gina felt moved to defend the Prince. 'I cannot but admire his taste in literature,' she protested. 'Is he not an admirer of Miss Austen's novels?'

'Oh, Gina, have you read it?' India's face lit up. 'Anthony has brought me a copy. It's called *Sense and Sensibility*. I'll be glad to lend it to you when I've finished it.'

'I'd like that. Miss Austen is a favourite with many people. They love the humour in her book. It is so subtle.'

'The Prince likes the Waverley novels too,' Thomas objected in gloomy tones. 'I tried one once. Couldn't get past the first page. All ancient history and prosing on as if we were still in the school-room...'

This brought cries of protest from the ladies and resulted in a heated discussion.

Gina glanced at her friend and was satisfied to see that her attempt at diversion had been successful. Some of the colour had returned to India's cheeks and she had lost the haunted look which was so troubling.

As she took her leave, Giles accompanied her to her carriage.

'Have you engagements for tomorrow?' he asked quietly.

Gina gave him a searching look before she answered. 'None that can't be broken,' she replied. 'Why do you ask?'

'I hoped…that is, I wondered if you would be good enough to visit India again. She is a different person in your company. I had not thought she would be so distressed by Isham's absence…'

'It is natural,' Gina comforted. 'And it is partly her condition. Fears can grow out of all proportion unless one gives another direction to one's thoughts.'

'That's true! Unfortunately, my mother adds to India's worries… I could wish that she would pay another visit to her friends….'

'Preferably far from here?' Gina twinkled at him.

'The farther the better!' He gave her an answering smile. 'Anthony can handle her, but my sisters are very much at her mercy.'

'And you?'

'I can't be here all day, Gina. Do say you'll come tomorrow…' He laid his hand upon her arm and Gina jumped as if she had been stung. Even through the fine cloth of her garments his touch had the power to set her senses aflame. Her eyes searched his face for some indication that his resolve was weakening, but Giles appeared to be thinking only of India.

'I'll come,' she promised as she stepped into her carriage.

On the journey back to Abbot Quincey she had much to occupy her mind. She could only rejoice that Giles had dropped his distant manner towards her. Now they were slipping back into the old comradeship which had first attracted them to each other. What had started as friendship had deepened into an overwhelming love. Could it do so again? In time of danger Giles must surely set aside his pride in the basic need to protect her and have her by his side. She prayed that it would be so.

Was she growing selfish? For these past few weeks she had been preoccupied with her own concerns, but now there were others to consider, apart from her own girls. It was a salutary thought.

With a lighter heart she hurried indoors, handing her spencer, her bonnet and her gloves to the waiting maid. If India needed diversion she should have it. Gina looked at her latest acquisition, the poems of Samuel Taylor Coleridge.

She and the girls had read 'The Ancient Mariner' and 'Kubla Khan' until they knew each word by heart. She chuckled to herself. How Mair and Elspeth had shuddered in mock horror as she had declaimed aloud!

Thomas Newby should be made to eat his words when he dismissed the whole of English literature. On the morrow she would make his blood run cold, and India would appreciate the joke.

There was Mrs Rushford to consider, of course. Gina rested her chin upon her hand. She could think of no immediate way of persuading India's mother to curb her foolish tongue. Perhaps the answer was to make some utterly outrageous statement in the hope of drawing her fire.

In the event, she had no need to do so. On the

following day she found the family gathered in the salon at the Grange. Having shaken off the effects of her sedative, Mrs Rushford was in full flow. She broke off to give Gina a sour look.

'I wonder that you dare to venture out, Lady Whitelaw. Had your husband been alive he would have forbidden it, I'm sure...'

'Fortunately, I am my own mistress, ma'am,' Gina said sweetly. 'As you see, I am unharmed.'

'Well, I suppose that you are accustomed to a certain lifestyle. My daughters have been brought up in a different way. They do not go racing about the countryside...'

Gina smiled, but she was aware that Giles had gone pale with anger. He was about to speak, but she shook her head at him. She had no wish to be the cause of a family quarrel.

'You have a letter, my lady.' India's butler held out a silver tray. 'There is also one for Mrs Rushford.'

'From Anthony?' India fell upon her letter with delight. 'Oh, please excuse me, but I must know what he has to say.' She scanned the missive quickly. Then she gave a sigh of relief. 'All is well,' she reported. 'There have been no more attacks. Bellingham is to be tried, but he has said nothing more.'

She looked round, smiling at her friends, but even as she did so the air was rent by a piercing scream.

'Mother, what is it?' Giles was across the room in a couple of strides. 'Are you ill?'

Speechless for once, Mrs Rushford shook her head.

'Then you can't have been listening to India. There seems to be no further danger to your safety…'

Feebly, she waved the piece of paper in her hand. 'Read that!' she gasped.

Five pairs of eyes were upon Giles as he scanned the single sheet. His reaction shocked them all. To everyone's surprise he gave a shout of laughter.

'Do share the joke!' India begged. 'We are all in need of entertainment.'

'And you shall have it!' Giles grinned at them, and then his face grew solemn. 'I am to be adopted,' he announced.

'Oh, Giles, don't gammon us! Won't you tell us what is in the letter?' Letty could not hide her curiosity.

'I've just told you. Mrs Clewes wishes me to take her name. She will then make me her heir.' His eyes were sparkling with amusement and the others refused to take him seriously.

'Wishful thinking, old fellow. Who could be so lucky?'

'It's true!' Mrs Rushford spoke in a hollow tone. 'Oh, my boy, who would have thought it?'

'Certainly not I. I hardly know the woman.'

'And I have never heard of her,' India announced. 'Where did you meet her, Giles?'

'At Bristol. We played cards with Lady Wells and her other cronies…'

'The demon gamblers?' Thomas raised an eyebrow. 'You must have made a great impression, Giles.'

'Giles was very kind to the old ladies,' his mother said with dignity. 'Mrs Clewes is not, perhaps, the type of person one would meet in the best society. She is extremely wealthy, so I understand, but her fortune comes from trade.'

'I liked her,' Giles said simply. 'There is no flummery about her.'

'I'm glad to hear it.' Mrs Rushford beamed upon him. 'My dear, your worries must now be at an end.'

The full import of this remark did not strike Giles at first. Then he became aware of the hush which followed it. He turned to face his mother.

'I hope I misunderstand you, ma'am.' His tone was incredulous. 'You can't possibly be suggesting that I give this offer serious consideration.'

'Consideration?' she snapped. 'Consideration? You should seize this opportunity with both hands. Where else will you come into possession of a fine competence? You will not wed to make your way in life...'

Thomas foresaw the coming storm. Excusing himself, he slipped quietly out of the room. His friend's face had grown dark with anger and he had no desire to witness a serious family quarrel.

Gina made as if to follow him, but Giles stopped her.

'Sit down, Gina!' he ordered. 'This concerns you too. Tell me, shall I accept this offer?'

It was against her own best interests, but Gina did not hesitate. 'You can't!' she said at once. 'You are the last of the Rushfords. You must not give up your name. It would be like selling it.'

'Indeed!' Mrs Rushford was beside herself with rage. 'And who are you, madam, to advise my son? Will you take him yourself and give him heirs?'

Giles took a step towards her, but India intervened. 'Mother, you have gone beyond the bounds of what is permissible,' she said in icy tones. 'Letty and I will take you to your room...'

It was enough to send Isabel Rushford into full hysterics. She screamed, sank to the floor, and began to drum her heels upon the carpet.

Giles took Gina's hand. 'Come into the study,' he said. 'My sisters know how to deal with this.'

'But can't I help?' she asked. 'I have had some experience.'

A grim smile touched his lips. 'I'm sure you have, but this is no case for a bucket of cold water, or a slap across the face. Knowing my mother, the doctor has left a supply of sedatives. The girls will settle her down.'

'I should not have been harsh,' she protested.

'I know it. I was teasing you, but you have every reason to resort to violence. I must apologise for my mother's words...'

'I believe she spoke without thinking,' Gina replied. 'It is understandable that she should consider your best interests as she sees them.'

'At any cost?'

Gina changed the subject. 'Tell me about this Mrs Clewes. Who is she, Giles, and how did you come to meet her?'

'Lady Wells invited us to Bristol when her son and

Letty wished to become engaged. As you can imagine, Oliver and Letty had eyes only for each other. I spent my time in playing cards with the other house guests. Mrs Clewes was one of them.'

'What type of person is she?'

To Gina's surprise, Giles twinkled at her. 'You'd like her. She's an original...'

'In what way?'

'Well, let me see... In the first place she makes no concessions to the present fashions, apart from a fondness for terrifying turbans. In the Grecian style, she informed me, she would resemble nothing so much as a sack of flour, knotted close to the neck.'

'She has a sense of humour then?'

'She has...and it can be withering. Sometimes I was hard put to keep my countenance. She has a way of catching one's eye when something ridiculous strikes her.'

'I can see why you would find her entertaining, but how does she come to be a guest of Lady Wells? Your mother mentioned that the lady's fortune came from trade. Is not Lady Wells a famous snob?'

'It *is* a mystery,' Giles admitted. 'Mrs Clewes may be a family connection of some sort. Lady Wells was forever trying to keep her in her room. Certainly she did not encourage private conversations with this particular guest.'

'But you must have spoken to her yourself.'

'Mrs Clewes and I had a number of assignations,' Giles said darkly.

Gina bridled. 'What age of woman is she?'

'She must be well into her seventies…widowed…and without an heir. I thought she seemed quite lonely.'

'And what was the purpose of these assignations?' Gina asked in a casual tone. At least, she hoped that she sounded casual.

Giles grinned at her. 'Mrs Clewes is fond of a glass of "flesh and blood". It is…er…was not available in her ladyship's household. I managed to get it for her.'

'Great heavens! What on earth is that?'

'It is a glass of port, well laced with gin. Don't be tempted to try it, Gina. I did myself. Believe me, it separates the men from the boys…!' He caught Gina's eye and they laughed until they were helpless.

'I see now why you are such a favourite with Mrs Clewes,' she teased.

'It wasn't entirely that.' Giles grew more serious. 'I found her to have a fund of what I can only describe as earthy common-sense. She isn't afraid to speak her mind.'

'I'm sorry that I won't meet her. What will you do now?'

'I'll write to her, of course, to thank her for her offer. If she is a connection of Lady Wells she might be persuaded to make Oliver her heir.'

Gina gave the suggestion her consideration. 'That might be best. Oliver is a younger son. He may not object to taking her name.' She paused. Then she asked the question that was uppermost in her mind.

'What did you mean when you said that this matter was of concern to me as well as to you?'

'Did I say that?' Giles looked at her in wonder. 'I needed your opinion, that was all.'

'Not quite all!' Gina was bitterly disappointed, but her expression gave no hint of it. 'There is something else which I should mention to you. Has Mr Newby told you that he offered for me?'

Giles nodded, sick with apprehension. Was she about to tell him that she'd changed her mind and would now accept his friend?

'Then you will know that I refused him. Under the circumstances I think it best if, for the present, you do not bring him to my home again. I'd like to avoid an awkward situation.'

She hoped he would accept the lame excuse, which was only partially true. If Giles persisted in treating her as a stranger she'd be in danger of breaking her heart for a second time, and that, she vowed, must not be allowed to happen. Better not to see him at all than to torture herself with vain hopes.

He made her a formal bow. 'As you wish,' he said. 'We shall not trouble you again.' He paused. 'You need not fear to visit India. We shall not be here.'

Chapter Ten

Giles kept his word to her, much to the disgust of Mair and Elspeth.

'But they promised!' both girls chorused.

Gina found that she was losing patience. 'You are no longer children,' she reproved. 'You must not behave as if some special treat has been denied to you. Both Giles and Mr Newby have been more than kind, but they have other calls upon their time.'

Then she looked at their downcast faces and relented. 'Cheer up!' she said. 'I plan to do more entertaining. You shall come down to dinner with our guests. Meantime we need to think about new gowns for you.' She picked up copies of *The Lady's Magazine* and *Ackermann's Repository* and left them absorbed in studying the latest fashions.

Her visit to India was brief that morning, and she was unsurprised to learn that plans for the subscription ball had been cancelled.

'I can't think it would be right to go ahead in the light of recent events,' India told her. 'Any celebration would be out of place in view of the assassination.'

'I agree, and people are still jittery. Have you more news from London?'

'Not much. There are no new developments, so Anthony tells me. The capital is fairly quiet, but the death of the Prime Minister has led to much rejoicing in the north.'

Gina changed the subject. 'How is Mrs Rushford?' she asked.

India gave her a faint smile. 'Subdued, I fear. She knows when she has gone too far with Giles.'

'Mrs Clewes's offer must have come as a shock to her,' Gina said kindly. 'Your mother had no time to consider the implications.'

'It's good of you to see it in that light, especially as she was so rude to you...'

Gina laughed. 'I often speak out of turn myself. I can't condemn it in others. When does Anthony return?'

'By Sunday at the latest, so he tells me. That wretched creature, Bellingham, is to be tried. If he's found to be insane, Anthony will try to save him, but he doesn't offer much hope.'

India's words were prophetic. When Isham returned a glance at his face told her the result of the trial. She did not question him, knowing that he would not care to distress her, but he spoke to Gina later.

'Is it all over?' she asked.

'Oh yes, justice has been served, or so the author-

ities would have us believe. Bellingham was tried
with indecent haste. The result was a foregone con-
clusion. He was executed in front of Newgate prison
in the midst of ugly scenes. The hangman was pelted
by the mob.'

Gina shuddered. 'When will they stop these public
executions?' she asked.

'That will come in time. For the present they are
regarded as a salutary deterrent. Now let us forget the
subject. I am in your debt, my dear, for the way you
have supported India. She has come to rely on your
good sense.'

'She has a great deal of her own,' Gina assured
him.

'That's true, but I worry about her, Gina. Her
mother attempts to fill her mind with fears.'

Gina was silent.

'Still the diplomat?' Isham smiled at her. 'Believe
me, I don't need your confirmation. I was concerned
before I left for London.'

Lost in thought he took a turn around the room. 'I
have a little plan,' he said at last. 'Sir James Perceval
and his wife are in London for Hester's season. Lady
Eleanor is sister to Mrs Rushford. I have an invitation
for Letty and her mother to join them. Do you think
that it will serve?'

'It's doubtful,' Gina told him. 'Mrs Rushford sees
an assassin behind every bush.'

'Then we must convince her otherwise. Bellingham
is dead, after all.'

'You might suggest that she spends her time in

choosing Letty's bride-clothes. That is, if…' She paused, but Isham understood her perfectly.

'She shall have a free hand,' he said at once. 'No expense will be too great if she can be persuaded to leave India's side. Will you help me?'

'I'll do my best,' she promised.

She wasted no time in setting about her task. In the event, Mrs Rushford needed little persuasion to undertake a trip to London, armed with rolls of bills in high denominations from her son-in-law and letters of credit drawn upon his bank.

Letty's shy objections were quickly waved aside.

'Are you out of your mind?' her mother demanded angrily. 'Here is Isham prepared to do his duty by you, as indeed he should, and you must make difficulties, you ungrateful girl!'

'I don't mean to be ungrateful, Mama, but shall I really need so much?' Letty thought with horror of the endless lists of proposed purchases drawn up by her mother. 'I mean…Anthony is paying all the expenses of my wedding…'

'And what has that to say to anything? Do you suppose that your brother-in-law can't afford it? Why, Letty, he is rich enough to buy an abbey. Besides, he told me himself that it would be his pleasure…'

Letty was reduced to silence, but she made it her business to seek out Isham in his study and thank him for herself.

'Nonsense!' he said warmly. 'If our roles were reversed would you not do the same for me?'

'That isn't very likely to happen.' Letty was forced to smile.

'Oh, I don't know,' he teased. 'I might invest in some dubious scheme and reduce myself to tramping the open road with India by my side. Do you suppose she would enjoy it?'

'With you, she would be happy anywhere, and under any conditions. You have made her so very happy, Anthony.'

For answer he kissed her cheek. 'Thank you, my dear. I wish the same for you and Oliver. Shall you see him when you are in London?'

Letty's face grew animated. 'Oh, yes. That is one reason why I have agreed…I mean…I don't like to leave India at this present time.'

'Letty, you will be doing me a service. You understand me? I think I need not say more. India must have peace of mind. You will oblige me by staying with your Aunt Eleanor for as long as possible.'

Letty understood him perfectly and she gave him a conspiratorial look.

'You and your mother need not fear the journey,' he continued. 'Giles and Thomas Newby will escort you.'

It was with a good deal of relief that he waved the little party off for London at the end of the following week. Then he ordered his horse brought round and set off for Abbot Quincey.

Gina welcomed him with unaffected pleasure. 'Is all well?' she asked.

'All is very well indeed,' he told her with mock solemnity. 'Today my prayers are answered. Isabel set off for London this very morning, with enough commissions to keep her occupied for weeks.'

Gina laughed aloud. 'Your plan worked then?'

'It did. I wish I could think of another. You don't suppose that she would care to live there permanently? I could take a house for her in some convenient part of the city.'

'You could suggest it,' Gina answered drily. 'She might agree to live with one of her bosom bows for companionship.'

'Are there any such?'

Gina laughed again. 'Now you are being unkind!' she accused.

'Sometimes I feel savage!' Isham said with feeling. 'And now she is at odds with Giles. He and Newby have gone with them, but he doesn't want to stay...' He glanced at Gina's face through half-closed lids, but her expression told her nothing.

'When will you come to see us, Gina? India has missed you these last few days.'

'I was being tactful,' she told him cheerfully. 'Now that you are returned from London, India has no need of anyone else.'

'She values her friends, my dear, and she looks forward to your visits.'

'Then I will come again tomorrow...' Secure in the knowledge that Giles would not return for several days, Gina was happy to agree.

Her resolution not to see him had not weakened,

but she missed him dreadfully. She'd tried to fill the gap by looking up old friends, but she and her child-hood playmates had grown too far apart.

Her household duties were quickly undertaken, leaving her time to read, to study, to choose plants for the new orangery, and to consider embellishing her wardrobe. She found that nothing could hold her interest.

More than anything she longed to feel that familiar leap of the heart whenever she saw Giles. Now she dwelt on every detail of that beloved face, loving the way his mobile mouth turned up at the corners when he smiled, the strong line of his jaw and the look in his blue eyes whenever she caught him unawares.

Giles was handsome, certainly, but she'd have loved him if he had been the ugliest man alive. They were soul-mates. If only he'd accept that the bond between them held them both for life.

She pushed the wish away. She had a pile of correspondence to attend to. Her friends in Scotland must not be neglected, but her stay there seemed to have taken place in another existence.

'Mr George Westcott, ma'am.' Hanson ushered her visitor into the room.

Gina turned with a welcoming smile. For the past two weeks her cousin had been her most frequent visitor. She was puzzled. Surely he did not share her parents' hope that she would wed him?

Had he shown any sign of making advances to her, she would have sent him to the rightabout, but George seemed to be content to be her friend.

This morning he seemed troubled.

'Is something wrong?' she asked.

'My father is returned to Abbot Quincey,' he said miserably.

'I see…and you are come to tell me that we shall be one more for dinner this evening?'

It was only with the greatest reluctance that Gina made this offer. Her uncle was not welcome in her home, but not to invite him would give rise to unwelcome comment.

'Not exactly!' George seemed unable to sit still. He rose and began to pace about the room. 'I haven't been honest with you, Gina. Haven't you wondered why I call on you so much?'

'I hoped it was because you enjoyed my company.' Gina prayed that he was not about to make a declaration.

'Well, I do, of course, but you see, I had to come. My father would have made enquiries, and I'm afraid for Ellie.'

Gina saw that he was in great distress. 'You had better tell me all about it,' she said quietly. 'I don't understand you, I'm afraid…'

George sat down then and poured out his story to her. 'It isn't that I don't like you, Gina,' he explained at last. 'But I love Ellie and I want to marry her.'

Gina thought for a moment. She had no doubt that Samuel Westcott would carry out his threat to harm the girl if his son did not obey him.

'It's time for some play-acting, George,' she said. 'This evening you must follow my lead, and remember, you must not laugh. That would give the game away…'

George looked mystified. 'I cannot come at your meaning, cousin…'

'I mean that you must make up to me. I promise to languish under your ardent gaze. I may even rest my head upon your shoulder…'

George looked startled. 'Would that not be doing it too brown?'

'Perhaps. We must keep it within the bounds of decorum… Are we agreed?'

'It would help to throw my father off the scent,' he admitted. 'It's the money, you see. He wants to keep it in the family…'

This bald statement was a severe trial to Gina's composure, but she kept her countenance.

'I didn't imagine that it was my delightful temperament, or my beautiful blue eyes,' she replied.

George stared at her, uncertain as to whether or not she was teasing, and Gina groaned to herself. Ellie, whoever she was, would find George heavy going unless she shared his lack of humour. Even so, she sympathised with him.

It would give her the greatest pleasure in the world to outwit her unpleasant uncle. He deserved a sharp set-down. Her only worry was that she might overplay her hand, but she thought she could judge her manner to a nicety.

The inclusion of her uncle had made them nine for dinner. He apologised for upsetting the arrangement of her table, but she made light of it. In a further blow to convention she seated George at her right hand.

Her brother exchanged a speaking glance with his wife, and her sister did the same. The Westcott brothers nodded and smiled at each other. Only Gina's mother eyed her daughter with some suspicion.

Gina affected not to notice. She kept the conversation light, chattering about her plans for the garden, and asking for advice from the assembled company.

'I plan a shrubbery, of course,' she said brightly. 'George, what do you think? Shall it be a circuit walk around the garden walls, in the serpentine style, or shall I plump for the theatrical? Mr Garrick had twin theatrical shrubberies in his Thames-side garden at Hampton House, you know.'

George did *not* know, and it was all too clear, but he made a manful effort.

'Cousin, I've always admired your taste,' he replied. 'Whatever you decide will be perfection, I am sure of it.'

'Too kind!' Gina replied in sentimental tones. Apparently without thinking she laid her hand on his and pressed it warmly. 'When it is finished we shall walk there. In Horace Walpole's words I plan ''odours beyond those of Araby''. It will be a haven of delight...'

George felt it was time to bring her down to earth. 'What plants will you choose?' he said.

Gina lavished an adoring look upon him. 'I thought of roses, pinks, honeysuckle and lilac among others. Are they your favourites too?'

George did not know a honeysuckle from a daffodil, but he did his best. 'I like snowdrops,' he said stoutly.

'Then we shall have those too, and other bulbs, as well as carnations and sunflowers. Oh, I can't wait to order all these treasures.'

'They'll cost you a pretty penny, my dear, but then, I suppose that is not of any concern to you...' Samuel Westcott seemed about to lick his lips. 'Tell me, where are your girls this evening?'

Gina gave him the briefest of looks, but it was enough. 'They are at dancing classes this evening,' she said. She did not miss his dreadful smile.

'Are they not over-young to be allowed out in an evening?' her mother said anxiously. 'You do not fear that they may be in danger?'

Privately, Gina considered that Mair and Elspeth were likely to be in more danger in her uncle's company, but she did not say so. He had a nasty habit of trapping young girls in passageways or hidden corners.

'They are in no danger outside this house.' Her look at her uncle was filled with meaning. 'I sent them in the carriage with two grooms for company...'

Samuel Westcott turned his head away and began to engage his brother in conversation.

'What do you say to this latest stab in the back?' he asked. 'I fear our trade will suffer even more.'

'The declaration of war by our former colonies? It isn't altogether unexpected. They've always resented our blockade of European ports, and they have no love for England.'

'We should have crushed that rebellion when we had the chance.' Samuel replied savagely. 'We should have sent more troops to the Americas. It's beyond belief that we could have been defeated by a rag, tag and bobtail of undisciplined farmers.'

'Yet they had something which our troops had not,' Gina observed. 'They were fighting for their belief in freedom. What was it they said; "No taxation without representation?" That sounded reasonable to me.'

Her uncle gave her a sour look. 'Much you women know about it, Gina! Leave it to those who understand these matters. Now they have invaded Canada. I regard that as the basest treachery. Our war with Napoleon has given them the chance they needed to strike when our backs were turned.'

Gina was about to reply when her mother caught her eye. As Mrs Westcott shook her head, Gina rose from the table.

'We'll leave you to your politics then,' she said as she led the ladies from the room.

Her mother took her to task at once. 'What can you be thinking of?' Mrs Westcott said severely. 'It's so unbecoming to put forward your opinions on matters which are of no concern to females.'

'Wars are of concern to everyone, Mother. Females have husbands and sons who may be called upon to fight. We cannot stick our heads in the sand like ostriches.'

Mrs Westcott sighed. 'You haven't changed, my dear. You were always such a forthright child. It will not do, you know. Gentlemen do not like it. Take care, or you will become known as a blue-stocking.'

Gina kissed her mother's cheek. 'Is that such a dreadful fate?' she teased.

'You may not think so, but I do. Poor George looked shocked.' She gave her daughter a sideways glance. 'How do you go on with him?'

'George is a dear. He calls on me quite often,' Gina told her truthfully. She was well aware that this item of information would be passed on to both the Westcott brothers, and she had promised to help George.

'George looks quite moonstruck,' her sister observed. 'Shall you wed him, Gina?'

'I hardly know him well enough as yet. Besides, I have no thought of marriage for the present.' Gina's look was demure. Hopefully, the three ladies would take it as a sign of interest in her cousin.

'I'm not surprised!' Her brother William's wife was undeceived. 'Why should you re-marry? You have money enough for all your needs. Why condemn yourself to submitting to a husband's wishes, producing a child each year?'

Mrs Westcott scowled at her daughter-in-law. 'There is such a thing as a woman's duty, Alice. William would not like to hear you speak so freely. Besides, Gina would like children of her own. She told me so herself.'

'That's true,' Gina said with perfect truth. 'But I must consider carefully. There is no hurry for the moment.'

'You won't be young for ever,' her sister snapped. 'The years will take their toll, as they have done for all of us.'

Gina looked at both Alice and Julia with new eyes. Each of them was close to her in age, but the casual observer would have guessed at a wider gap. Discontent was evident on each face and the reason was not far to seek. They envied her her money and her freedom.

She tried for a lighter touch. Gossip was a favourite topic of conversation in all the Abbey villages.

'Do you hear anything of the Marchioness of Sywell?' she asked.

As she had hoped this brought immediate response from all three of her companions. They vied with each other to bring her up to date with all that had happened at the Abbey since she left.

'You'd be too young to understand the implications when the Earl of Yardley lost the Abbey to Sywell,' Mrs Westcott told her. 'That was the start of the trouble.'

'But I do remember something about it, Mother. We children sang silly songs about it at the time. Did not the Earl of Yardley lose the Abbey in a gambling session? Then he blew his brains out?'

'It was a tragedy, Gina. The Earl had had a serious quarrel with his son. Something about the Viscount's wish to marry a French Catholic, I believe. His father cut him off, but when Lord Rupert was reported killed in Paris the Earl was distraught. He almost drank himself insensible whilst gambling. In the end he lost everything to Sywell, and then he killed himself.' Mrs Westcott shuddered. 'He could not have imagined what we would get in his place.'

'I don't know much about Sywell,' Gina admitted. 'He is not seen in Abbot Quincey…'

'He durst not show his face,' Julia told her. 'For years he and his cronies regarded the village girls as fair game. Orgies were the least of it. He has ruined not only the girls, but also some of the tradesmen. He does not settle his accounts, and no one will deliver to the Abbey now, and none of the villagers will work there.'

'So how does he manage to live?'

'One man has stayed with him. His name is Burneck. He is some kind of valet cum general servant. Occasionally he hires domestics in town, but they don't stay long.'

'And yet the Marquis married?' Gina said in wonder. 'The girl was very young, so I understand…'

'She was little more than a child, my dear. Heaven knows what pressure was brought to bear upon her to cause her to accept that monster. Now she has disappeared.'

'I shouldn't be the least surprised if the Marquis has done away with her,' Alice insisted. 'He's capable of anything.'

'But not of murder, surely?' Gina was shocked.

'Why not? I can't think of a crime which cannot be laid at his door.'

'She may have found her life intolerable. Perhaps she ran away…?'

'Perhaps!' Alice was unwilling to give up her belief in the ultimate perfidy. 'How I wish that the man would sell the Abbey and move elsewhere!'

'The Earl of Yardley has tried to buy back the Abbey,' Mrs Westcott told her. 'It would be a great relief to all of us to have the original family back again.'

'But Sywell will not sell?'

'No, Gina. He takes a perverse pleasure in taunting the Earl.'

'But I thought that Yardley killed himself?'

'The present Earl is a relative. He made his fortune in India and purchased land from his cousin, the Earl of Yardley. With Yardley and Lord Rupert dead, he inherited the title.'

'If Sywell is in debt, he may change his mind.'

'I doubt it. Sywell would cut off his nose to spite his face for the opportunity of doing an injury to one of his erstwhile friends.'

'He sounds delightful!' Gina said drily. 'Let us not lose hope! Someone may decide to remove him from the face of the earth...'

Her remark was made half in jest, but within a week her wish was granted.

Gina was in the garden, leafing through a book of poems by Robert Southey, when her visitors were announced.

Her heart was in a turmoil as Giles strode across the lawn towards her. His visit was unexpected, and she could think of no reason for it, but it was more than welcome. Her good resolutions vanished like snow in summer as she rose to her feet and held out both her hands.

He took them swiftly. 'There's been another murder,' he said without preamble. 'Sywell was found dead this morning.'

'The Marquis? Is this the work of the Luddites, Giles?'

'I doubt it. Sywell was no threat to them. He owned no factories, and had no interest in the introduction of new machinery.'

'How was he killed?'

'Stabbed through the heart, but his valet found no sign of an intruder.'

'I'm not surprised. The Abbey is a warren of passages and hiding places.' Gina thought for a moment. 'It must have been someone who knew the place, and how to reach Sywell's rooms. A casual thief would find that difficult.'

'There's sure to be a serious investigation,' Giles continued. 'The Runners have been summoned, but if I'm not mistaken the Regent will wish his own men to take charge. The murder of a peer of the realm cannot be ignored.'

Thomas Newby intervened. 'I don't see why not,' he objected. 'The fellow was a monster.'

'Even so, the Regent will consider it an unfortunate precedent. Allow the murder of a member of the aristocracy to go unpunished, and our unfortunate Prince may be the next victim. He's one of the most unpopular men in England.'

Neither of his companions was prepared to argue with this statement.

'So many people hated Sywell.' Gina mused. 'One might as well look for a particular straw in a hay-stack.'

'His widow is a favourite candidate,' Giles told her grimly. 'She will inherit the Abbey...'

'And a mountain of debt,' Gina objected. 'Besides, she hasn't been seen for months...'

'She may not have gone far. If she planned the murder she would lie low, awaiting a suitable oppor-tunity. She would know the Abbey well, you must agree.'

'But women don't often resort to stabbing, Giles. In the first place it requires great physical strength to overpower a man, unless she attacked him whilst he was sleeping. I'm told that the Marchioness was a slender, gentle creature. I doubt if she would be ca-pable of violence.'

'We can't know what her life was like before she left the Marquis. She may have been driven to des-peration.'

'That's more than likely,' Thomas agreed. 'We all knew Sywell's reputation, but I agree with Lady Whitelaw. Poison is more of a woman's weapon.'

'Thank you, Mr Newby!' Gina's tone was dry. 'I see that you think highly of us as a sex.'

'I do, ma'am, as you know!' He gave her a look of such blatant adoration that Gina was nonplussed. Irony, she decided, was quite lost on Thomas.

'There must be other suspects,' she suggested. 'The

fathers and brothers of the girls the Marquis ruined must be high on the list, and some of his bastards too will be old enough to take revenge…'

She heard a gasp from Thomas, and guessed correctly that he was unused to such plain speaking from a woman.

'It could be one of Sywell's gambling cronies,' he said hastily. 'He's thought to have ruined many a man and not always by fair means…'

Giles had been silent for some time. 'There is always Burneck himself, of course,' he said at last. 'What better way to hide his guilt than to raise the alarm and set the countryside by the ears…?'

'I can't believe that,' Gina objected. 'Burneck has stayed by his master's side all these years. Why should he resort to murder now?'

'There could be a number of reasons…perhaps a promised legacy withdrawn, or something of that sort.'

'Possibly!' Gina was unconvinced. 'You still think that the Luddites are not to blame?' She had kept up a brave face, but the strain of this latest news was beginning to tell, and she had grown pale. She sat down in the nearest chair and hid her shaking hands within her skirts.

Giles was beside her in an instant. 'My dear, I have been thoughtless,' he said tenderly. 'I should not have troubled you with this dreadful story.'

Gina shook her head. The solicitude in his voice brought her close to tears, but she blinked them away.

'I'm glad you let me know,' she whispered. 'It is

just that… Oh, Giles, there has been so much violence in these past few weeks. First the murder of Isham's half-brother at the Grange, and the riots. Then the assassination of the Prime Minister, and now this… Are we on the verge of revolution? It happened in France not twenty years ago.'

'It couldn't happen here,' Thomas said with conviction.

'Don't be too sure,' she murmured. 'Are we too squeamish a nation to rely on the headsman's axe? We executed our own king, if I recall.'

Giles slipped a comforting arm about her shoulders. 'Do you trust Isham, Gina?'

She nodded wordlessly.

'Then come back to the Grange with us. Talk to him. The Government keeps him up to date with all the latest news. He is convinced that there will be no revolution here. This murder is a local tragedy. He is sure of it.'

Gina allowed herself to be persuaded into visiting the Grange, ostensibly to be reassured by Isham. In reality, she was conscious of a very feminine need to cling to Giles for support. It was ridiculous, she told herself sharply. What had happened to the strong-willed Gina Westcott, with her ability to handle any situation? The character of that iron lady seemed to have changed beyond recognition.

She had expected to find India in a similar state of shock, but to her surprise her friend looked perfectly serene.

India glanced at Gina's troubled face and hurried

to embrace her. 'Come and sit down,' she said gently. 'This murder is a dreadful thing, my dear, but Anthony is convinced that it is the result of some private feud.'

Isham himself confirmed her words. 'There is no talk of general insurrection, Gina, but if you are still worried why not bring the girls and stay with us?'

His wife gave him a smile of thanks. 'That might be best. We have room and to spare now that my mother and Letty are gone to London. Lucia, Anthony's step-mama, went with them.'

Gina recovered some of her composure. 'You are very kind,' she said quietly. 'But I couldn't think of it. I don't know why I've allowed the news of the murder to upset me so. I didn't even know the Marquis, but I seem to be on edge these days.'

Isham could have made a shrewd guess as to the reason but he let it pass. At the sound of carriage wheels he strolled over to the window.

'It seems we have a visitor,' he announced. 'Giles, is this anyone you know?' He was unprepared for his brother-in-law's reaction.

'Great heavens!' Giles had stiffened. 'As I live and breathe! It's Mrs Clewes!'

Chapter Eleven

As their visitor was announced, five pairs of eyes focused upon her in astonishment.

Mrs Clewes was an amazing sight. She was very short and almost as wide as she was tall. In an effort to add inches to her stature she sported an aigrette-topped turban in a particularly violent shade of blue. This clashed in the most painful way with the gown which could be glimpsed beneath her travelling cloak.

It was clear that the lady made no concession to the present fashion for simple Grecian styles. Panniers held out her voluminous skirts, beneath which could be seen an ancient pair of carpet slippers.

At first it seemed unlikely that she would manage to negotiate the doorway, but with the ease born of long practice she turned sideways, swept into the room, and waddled towards the waiting company.

Isham was the first to recover his sang-froid. With his customary courtesy he moved towards his guest.

'Welcome, ma'am!' he bowed. 'It is Mrs Clewes, is it not?'

'It is!' Mrs Clewes was perfectly at ease. 'You'll be Isham, I expect, and Letty's brother-in-law?'

Isham bowed again. 'May I present my wife, and Lady Whitelaw, who is a friend of ours. This is Mr Thomas Newby, and Giles you already know.'

'Aye! He's the lad I've come to find. How do you go on, my dear?'

Giles came towards her then and took her out-stretched hands, smiling as he did so.

'Ma'am, I am well,' he said. 'No need to ask how you go on. You are the picture of health…'

'Flatterer! I expect you must be wondering why I'm here?'

'Before you tell us, Mrs Clewes, will you not take a comfortable chair?' Isham led her forward. 'You must have found your journey tiring. Allow me to offer you some refreshment…' He rang the bell.

'I won't deny I'll be glad to take the weight off my feet, my lord.' Mrs Clewes settled herself with a gusty sigh. 'I ain't as young as I used to be.'

'And what is your pleasure, ma'am? Some wine, perhaps?'

It was at this point that Giles intervened. 'Mrs Clewes believes a glass of "flesh and blood" to be the best restorative,' he said solemnly.

'Then "flesh and blood" it is. Tibbs, will you see to it?'

'Certainly, my lord.' Tibbs did not betray his aston-ishment by the flicker of an eyelid, nor did he need to ask the nature of this tipple. It was a favourite of his own, though to his knowledge it had not been served before in the salon at the Grange.

'Well now, I won't take up your time,' Mrs Clewes announced. 'I came to have a word with Mr Rushford here.'

'A private word, ma'am? If so, may I offer you my study?'

'Not unless Giles insists, my lord. I have a bone to pick with him, you know.'

Giles had suspected something of the kind. Mrs Clewes had greeted him kindly enough, but it was possible that she had been mortally offended by his refusal to take her name.

'You may say anything to me in front of my family,' he told her. 'Believe me, ma'am, when I wrote to you I had no intention of insulting you.'

A crackle of amusement greeted his words. 'It would take a better man than you to do that, my lad.' Mrs Clewes sipped at her drink with great appreciation. 'I didn't expect you to accept. At least, I hoped you wouldn't.'

Giles stared at her.

'Surprised? I can see you are. You passed the test, my dear. Stiff-necked you may be, but you ain't a hypocrite…'

'I'm afraid I don't follow you, ma'am.'

'Dear me! What an innocent it is! Did it not strike you as strange that I should offer to make you my heir when Leah's children have first call upon my purse?'

'You refer to Lady Wells?'

'She is my niece, Giles, though she don't care to acknowledge it. Still, I suppose that we've all got skeletons in the cupboard.'

The thought of regarding Mrs Clewes as a skeleton tried the composure of her listeners sorely, but no one smiled.

'Then why did you make me such an offer, ma'am?'

'Well, I'll tell you. First of all, I ain't accustomed to being treated like a lady, and you was always kind to me. I'm something of a judge of men, but for all I knew you could have had an eye to the main chance.'

Giles stiffened.

'Now, my lad, don't get upon your high ropes! You wouldn't be the first as has tried to take me in.'

'I'm sure that you are not easily deceived, Mrs Clewes…' Giles could not hide his anger.

'No, I'm not, but I had to be sure…'

'For what reason, ma'am?' India was intrigued.

'Why, my dear, this brother of yours has a fortune in his hands, if he would but make use of it.'

'You are mistaken, madam. I have nothing.'

'And whose fault is that, you stubborn creature? It's high time that you set about making use of these inventions of yours. I've spoken to my man of business and he agrees with me.'

'You are interested in farming methods, Mrs Clewes?' Isham was beginning to enjoy himself.

'Not a bit of it, my lord, but I'm interested in making money. Clewes was my third, and he left me comfortable, but I don't turn up my nose when I see the chance of a profit.'

'Your third?' India was bewildered.

'My third husband, My Lady. I've buried three by now. The first two were no fools but Clewes was a ship's chandler at Bristol. He taught me to use my head.'

'I have no doubt of that,' Isham smiled at her. 'How can Giles help you, ma'am?'

'I want him to be my partner. I can afford to back him for a start and then we'll share the profits. The books won't be no trouble to me. I'll see he don't get into queer street.'

Isham forebore to mention that he had already offered to help Giles. He awaited the outcome of this latest suggestion with interest. If he were any judge the redoubtable Mrs Clewes would have her way no matter what the opposition from her unwilling partner.

Incensed, Giles was about to refuse the offer outright. Then, as he looked at the dumpy little figure looking so out of place in the splendid salon he saw that her bright blue eyes were pleading with him.

'Are we not friends?' she said. 'We deal so well together, you and I. We'll be good partners...'

He swallowed his pride. 'You don't understand, I fear, my dear ma'am. There may be no profits. I should not care to be the cause of you suffering heavy losses.'

'Nay, lad, I'm not a fool. I've gone into the matter, and I've brought some papers with me. You'll look at them, at least? Who knows, with the cost of living rising as it does, this may be my chance to enjoy a comfortable old age…'

Mrs Clewes assumed a mournful expression and seemed to shrink into her chair…the picture of an elderly lady on the verge of poverty.

Isham hid a smile. It was a masterful performance. He was beginning to understand why other offers of help had failed. Giles would not accept them on his own behalf, but when asked to be of service to another human being he might yet be persuaded to agree.

'Allow me to send refreshment into the study for you,' he begged. 'You will both wish to study these papers at your leisure.'

Mrs Clewes struggled out of her chair. 'Give me your arm,' she said to Giles. 'If nothing else you can tell me all your news.'

To refuse her would have been out of the question and with a rueful smile Giles led her from the room.

'Good heavens, what a character!' India was stunned. 'Gina, what do you think of her?'

'I think her a very clever woman. If I'm not mistaken she will twist Giles round her little finger.'

'Nothing is more certain,' Isham agreed. 'And high time too. Newby, has Giles said nothing to you about his friendship with Mrs Clewes?'

'He told me that they played cards together.' Thomas was still in a state of shock. 'But they played for pennies. He had no idea at the time that she had a handsome fortune.'

'Perhaps she is not so very wealthy,' India offered. 'She seemed concerned about her future.'

'A subterfuge, my love. You did not see her carriage or her horses. They are the finest that money can buy.'

'And didn't you notice her necklace, India? I've seen rubies such as those in India. They are worth a king's ransom.' Gina was in a torment, hoping against hope that Giles would seize this opportunity so readily offered to him. She would have given much to have heard the discussion taking place at that very moment in the study.

It lasted for more than an hour, but when Mrs Clewes and Giles rejoined them she knew at once that they had reached agreement.

'Then we must celebrate your partnership.' Isham rang for wine, and Mrs Clewes was happy to accept yet another glass of her favourite 'flesh and blood', which appeared to have not the slightest effect upon her.

'Where are you staying, ma'am?' India asked politely.

'I've put up at the Angel, my lady. It seemed the best that the village has to offer.'

'But shall you be comfortable there? You are welcome to stay with us, if you should care to do so.'

'Bless your kind heart, my dear! I shouldn't like to trouble you…'

'Madam, it would be a pleasure.' Isham was at his most gallant. 'We are sadly short of company at present, and Lady Whitelaw has refused us. My wife would welcome a change of conversation. She does not go out at present.'

'Are you increasing, my lady? No signs yet, I see, and the first months are always the worst.'

'You have children of your own, Mrs Clewes?' India had warmed to the old lady.

'I lost my boys in the wars, my dear. One was with Nelson's navy and the other was with Wellington. Your brother ain't unlike my eldest lad.'

This admission told the company much about the unexpected offer to Giles. He came to her then and sat beside her.

'Will you stay with us?' he begged. 'I'll be happy to fetch your things from the Angel.'

'You are too good!' She patted his hand. 'I won't get in the way if you have visitors.'

'You will be our honoured guest,' Isham said at once. He looked up as Tibbs announced nuncheon, and offered Mrs Clewes his arm to lead her into the dining-room.

India smiled at Gina. 'Anthony is much taken with our guest...'

'I'm not surprised,' came the quick reply. 'She's such a good-hearted, straight-talking woman. I should not care to try to hide a secret from her though.' Gina had noticed how the lady's birdlike glance had rested on each of her companions in turn without appearing to do so. She had studied Gina for somewhat longer than the others, but it was some days before she attempted to engage her in private conversation.

The weather had improved, and now all the talk

was of Lady Eleanor's annual fête at Perceval Hall. It was the highlight of the year for the local villagers and all were welcomed with unlimited food and drink.

Gina paid her promised daily visits to the Grange, but she saw little of Giles. She was aware that he and Mrs Clewes had journeyed into Northampton to sign the partnership agreement. Since then the lady had wasted no time. She produced a short list of possible customers and sent Giles off without delay to demonstrate his inventions.

'Missing him?' she enquired one day. She and Gina were alone in the salon.

'I beg your pardon, ma'am?' Gina was startled out of her usual composure.

'I ain't referring to Mr Newby and well you know it, young woman.' Mrs Clewes gave a comfortable chuckle. 'Did you think I hadn't guessed that you're the one for Giles?'

To her own annoyance Gina felt her colour rising. 'You are quite mistaken, Mrs Clewes. Giles Rushford has no thought of me.'

'Bless my soul, Lady Whitelaw, are you blind? He thinks of nothing else, apart from his inventions. When he enters a room he looks for you, and you won't tell me that you don't feel the same. When you are together there is something in the air which cannot be mistaken.'

Gina shook her head. 'I beg your pardon, ma'am but that must be only in your imagination…'

'I ain't got one, Lady Whitelaw. I look only for hard facts…'

'Well, then, the fact is that I haven't exchanged a word with Giles for days.'

'How can you when he ain't here?'

This reasonable statement brought a smile from Gina.

'That's better!' her inquisitor announced. 'You may think I'm a bossy old woman, too fond of interfering, but I have grown to love that young man. I want only what will make him happy, and I think you feel the same. Isn't that so?'

Gina nodded. She could not trust herself to speak. Her lips were quivering and she was very close to tears.

'There now, don't upset yourself.' The older woman patted her hand. 'Give the man time. You've waited for ten years…another week or two won't make much difference.'

'Oh, he should not have told you…' Gina cried in anguish.

'He didn't. There was no need. I saw that there was something wrong when I first met him. It wasn't on the surface, of course. Giles was always the perfect gentleman, but it ain't natural for a man of thirty to be so grave beyond the likes of other men.'

'His life has not been easy,' Gina ventured.

'No more than many another. There was something else. To me it seemed to be a loss of a more serious kind. Giles had had a crushing blow in his youth. I made it my business to discover what had happened.'

'You couldn't have found it easy.'

'I didn't, but I'm a sharp one, Lady Whitelaw. I

pieced it all together. Then, when I met you, I had the final piece of the puzzle.'

'Ma'am, you are very shrewd,' Gina blinked away her tears. 'But now you, you know, with this splendid offer…this partnership of yours…he could have said something. Until now, he felt that the difference in our fortunes was too great.'

'Stiff-necked crittur! Don't despair, my dear. All will be well. He'll come back with more orders than he can fulfil…'

'You seem very sure of that.'

'Aren't you? When Giles believes in something he can be persuasive… Besides, he's working now to prevent me from sinking into a poverty-stricken old age.'

She gave a hearty laugh, and after a moment Gina joined her.

'Mrs Clewes, I believe you are what is known as a card,' she accused.

'Well, my dear, I've had three husbands. Rushing on like a bull at a gate ain't always the wisest course. Sometimes it takes a bit more cunning to set a man to rights.'

'I'll bear that in mind,' Gina promised. On impulse she kissed her companion gently on the cheek. 'I admire you so much,' she said.

The small gesture of affection succeeded in putting her companion quite out of countenance.

'Bless me, ma'am, there's no call for you to make a fuss of me.' For once Mrs Clewes was flustered, and Gina saw that her eyes were wet. 'You'll turn me into a watering-pot. I ain't used to it.'

'Then you shall grow used to it,' Gina promised. 'Tell me, ma'am, shall you attend the fête at Perceval Hall?'

Mrs Clewes shook her head. 'T'wouldn't be right, my dear. I'd gather a bigger crowd than the coconut shies...' Something in her voice made Gina look a question. To her horror she saw a look of pain in the older woman's eyes.

'You think I don't know what I look like?' her companion challenged. 'Why, 'tis only you and this family who don't regard me as some kind of freak.'

'No one who knows you could possibly think that, my dear ma'am. You could dine with me before the fête, and we could go together...'

It took some persuasion, but when Gina included the rest of the Isham family and Thomas Newby in her invitation Mrs Clewes agreed at last. She beamed as India joined them.

'Well, my lady, what does the doctor have to say to you?' she asked.

'He's pleased, and so am I now the sickness does not trouble me in a morning. It will be a relief to be able to go about again without the need to rush away at times.'

''Tis a trial, my dear, but worth it in the end. When you have your babe you'll forget the discomfort of these months.'

'I'm sure of it. I feel so well at present.'

'I'm glad to hear it, my dear one.' Isham had entered the room, accompanied by Thomas Newby. 'You will be the belle of the fête and carry off all the prizes.'

'I doubt that, Anthony,' India smiled up at her husband. 'But I shall be glad to see so many of my friends again, and most especially Hester... My cousin was always so full of news. I've missed her since she went to London for her Season.'

'Today I hope to prove a worthy substitute, my darling. I too have news. As we expected, the murder of the Marquis is to be investigated by the Prince Regent's men. They are already in the village.'

'Murder!' Mrs Clewes echoed blankly. 'You've had a murder here in Abbot Quincey?'

'My dear ma'am, don't distress yourself. It happened before you arrived here.' Isham was quick to reassure his guest. 'We had no wish to worry you with the story, though I doubt that you will have heard of the victim...the Marquis of Sywell?'

'Oh, I've heard of him, my lord. Show me someone who don't know of his goings-on. We shouldn't speak ill of the dead, I know, but ain't you well rid of him?'

'That is the general opinion, ma'am, but murder cannot be condoned.'

Unrepentant, Mrs Clewes began to chuckle. 'You may be right. We'd be knee deep in corpses otherwise. I can think of a few prime candidates for murder.'

'That's a blood-thirsty statement if ever I heard one.' Giles stood in the doorway grinning cheerfully at the assembled company. 'I must hope that you don't intend to put it into practice, Mrs Clewes?'

'Don't think I ain't considered it at times,' Mrs Clewes beamed at her new-found partner. 'The trouble is I ain't no shot and I can't run fast enough to catch a villain to strangle him...'

'You can't think how relieved I am to hear it.' Giles was laughing openly as he came to her and took her hands, kissing them both in turn.

'Get on with you! You don't believe a word of it! Now how did you fare, my lad? Do we have an order?'

'We have as many as we can handle, ma'am, with others promised for the future...'

There was a general murmur of congratulation as Giles listed his successes. Gina could only marvel at the change in him. His journey had been long that day but he seemed so fresh, so alert, and so alive.

Suddenly she felt unaccountably nervous. With the coming change in his fortunes Giles would be free to offer for her, but would he do so? The uncertainty was unbearable. At the first opportunity she excused herself and left for Abbot Quincey.

On the journey home she took herself to task. Her departure from the Grange had been sudden to the point of rudeness. What must the Ishams think of her? Good manners indicated that she should have stayed to join in the celebrations. Instead, she recalled muttering something about a forgotten appointment. It was a lame excuse, which would not have deceived a child.

She clenched her hands until the nails dug into her palms. She would make amends when she felt calmer. What she needed was time to think.

Her wish seemed unlikely to be granted.

'You have a visitor, Ma'am,' her butler announced as she walked into the hall.

George again? Gina sighed to herself. She had no wish to listen to her cousin's lamentations at that particular moment.

'You should have denied me,' she snapped more sharply than was her wont. 'You knew that I was not at home.'

'I tried, ma'am, but the gentleman would not be denied. He said that you were to be expected within minutes...'

Was George spying on her? Indignantly, Gina stalked into the salon. Then she stopped. It was Giles who came towards her.

'How did you get here?' she whispered. 'I left you at the Grange...'

'You did indeed! Why did you run away, my darling? You must have known that I would wish to speak to you.'

'How could I know that? You've spent these last few weeks in trying to avoid me...' Gina could not hide her hurt and disappointment.

Giles had come towards her with outstretched arms, but now they fell to his sides. 'I can only ask for your forgiveness, Gina. I've been a selfish fool, thinking only of my pride...my honour. Send me away if you

must, but believe me when I tell you that I've come
to my senses at last.'

'And what has caused this sea-change, sir?' Gina
was determined that she would not make the same
mistake again. Giles would not find her ready to fall
into his arms.

'Long ago I wanted to offer you the world,' he
answered sadly. 'I found I couldn't even give you part
of it.'

'And what made you think that I wanted the whole
world?' she asked coldly. 'Did I ever ask for it?'

'No, you didn't. I know your loving heart. You
would have suffered anything with me.'

'There we differ, Giles. You could not put aside
your pride for me.'

'Would you have had me do so? I think I could
bear anything but your pity and contempt...'

'Contempt?'

'Oh yes, it might have come to that, my dear. How
could I live upon your fortune, knowing that I had
done nothing to earn a comfortable life?'

Gina kept her eyes fixed firmly on the carpet. 'You
must have ridden hard to outpace my cattle, Giles.
Will you allow me to offer you refreshment?'

'Damn the refreshment!' he shouted explosively.
'Why do you think I'm here?'

'I haven't the least idea, but I'd be obliged if you
would refrain from swearing...'

'You'd make a saint swear, Gina, and I'm no saint.'

'That I can believe. For once we are in complete
agreement...' Gina's shoulders were shaking.

'Why you little minx, you are gammoning me!' Without more ado Giles took her in his arms. 'If you weren't so adorable I swear I'd put you across my knee...'

'You could try,' she agreed. 'Have you forgotten my fearsome reputation?'

'I have forgotten nothing...' As his lips found hers the long years of heartbreak faded as if they had never been. The lovers were transported in an instant back to that terrace in Italy where they had vowed eternal love.

When Giles released her at last, Gina clung to him, half laughing and half crying.

'Can this be true?' she whispered. 'I'd almost given up hope that we'd find happiness together...'

'And I! Why do you think I never married, Gina? I hadn't forgotten my vows to you, although it seemed impossible that we should ever meet again.' His mouth came down on hers once more, urgent, demanding and yet filled with tenderness.

'I'd almost decided to go away again...' she told him breathlessly. 'Oh, my darling, would you have let me leave you if you had not had this offer from Mrs Clewes?'

He shook his head. 'Not this time. I would have found some way, even if it had meant asking you to wait... But it was Mrs Clewes who brought me to my senses.'

'She's been a good friend to you...'

'And to you, my love. That morning in the library she gave me a tongue-lashing which I won't forget.

She has a flaying turn of phrase, you know. I felt lucky to escape with a whole skin. I was given a full account of the failings of my character.'

'Perhaps you'd better tell me,' she teased. 'Before I commit myself to a life of misery with a monster.'

His arms tightened about her, and the smile vanished from his lips. 'I wonder that you can be so generous, Gina. I have behaved in a monstrous way, I know. Mrs Clewes left me in no doubt that in refusing offers of help I was thinking only of myself. She left nothing unspecified, and I had no difficulty in recognising the miserable creature she described.'

Gina kissed his cheek. 'It was all said in love, my dear. She is so fond of you. She thinks only of your happiness.'

'I don't deserve either of you,' he said simply. 'Women are amazing creatures. Who would care for an arrogant, stiff-necked fellow, eaten up with pride, and full of self-pity…?'

She raised her fingers to his lips to hush the bitter words. 'No!' she said. 'I won't have that. We both knew you to be an honourable man, and we understood your need for self-respect. Would Mrs Clewes have offered you this partnership if she had not been sure of your honesty? And would I have loved you for so long?'

With a muffled groan he caught her to him again. 'Darling Gina, what can I say to you? If I have failings, you have none.'

Gina chuckled. 'Don't believe it, my dear one. Impulsive, hot-tempered and impatient of convention—

I am all of these things. Shall I go on, or shall we agree that we are fallible human beings?'

He silenced her by raining kisses on her hair, her cheeks, her eyelids and her throat.

'When can we be wed?' he asked. 'Will you keep me waiting, Gina?'

She looked at him with misty eyes. Then she shook her head. 'It shall be whenever you wish, my love.'

With a shout of joy he seized her hand. 'Come back to the Grange with me. Let us share our happiness with the others. Isham will tell me how to get a special licence, though I expect it will be a shock to him…'

To his surprise, this didn't prove to be the case.

'We wondered only what was taking you so long,' Isham observed with twinkling eyes. 'You've been a shocking slow-coach, my dear chap. Gina might have been carried off by half-a-dozen men.'

'And I was one of them.' Thomas came forward to kiss her hand and congratulate his friend, wishing them both all happiness.

He left them then to return within the hour with Mair and Elspeth.

'Mr Newby is so mysterious,' Elspeth cried as she rushed into the room. 'He's promised us a surprise, but he won't tell us what it is.'

'I can guess,' Mair said quietly as she looked at Gina's face. 'You are going to marry Giles?'

'Bless me if the child ain't a witch!' Mrs Clewes

beamed happily at the assembled company. 'How did you guess, my dear?'

Mair blushed. 'I saw the way he looked at Gina when he thought she wasn't watching.'

Giles gave her a bear hug. 'You are a dangerous woman, Mair. Remind me to be more circumspect when I want to keep a secret.'

This brought a ripple of amusement from his companions.

'A secret?' India teased. 'You have been mooning about like a lovesick calf these many months...'

Giles looked disconcerted for a moment. Then he began to smile.

'Families!' he said in mock disgust. 'Gina, what are we to do with them?'

'For a start you might invite us to your wedding,' India suggested. 'When is it to be?'

'As soon as possible,' he told her promptly. 'Gina has promised not to keep me waiting. All we need now is a special licence...'

'But, my dear brother, what of Mama and Letty? You'll wait until they return from London?'

'And when is that to be?' he asked impatiently.

'They plan to be back in time for the fête at Perceval Hall...'

'But that is weeks away...' he protested.

Gina laid a hand upon his arm. 'India is right, my darling. We can't think only of ourselves. Your mother would be heartbroken not to see you wed... Besides, there are matters to attend... I must buy my gown...'

This wasn't strictly true. Gina had no vanity. She would have been happy to be married in her oldest gown, but she guessed that Giles would accept her explanation.

He did so with a rueful sigh. 'Am I to be outvoted then?'

'Always where the ladies are concerned, my dear fellow...' Isham was smiling broadly. 'Take heart! At least you will not need a special licence. There is time for the banns to be called in the usual way.'

Giles did not argue further, but later, when they were alone, he held Gina to his heart, stroking her hair and kissing her hands by turns.

'You are very silent,' she whispered.

'That's because I can't believe that you are to be mine at last. Do dreams come true, my love?'

'Mine have done so, Giles. I never gave up hope completely, even when it seemed that all hope was gone. You are all I want in life...'

He kissed her then with a passion that spoke of years of longing, and Gina clung to him, offering him her heart and soul.

'I wonder if you have any idea how much I love you?' he said at last. 'I swear I'll make you happy, Gina. Nothing and no one shall ever harm you from now on.'

'Is that a challenge to fate?' Laughing, she threw her arms about his neck. 'Perhaps I should have my fortune told. Do you fear dark forces in my future?'

'Nothing shall ever injure you, my darling...'

'Of course it won't,' she said with happy certainty. 'I have no enemies, my dear.'

Chapter Twelve

Gina spent the following weeks in a daze of happiness. She seemed to be living in another world, where every sense was heightened. Suddenly, she felt like a girl again, for the sensation was familiar from those long-ago days when she and Giles had first fallen in love.

Now she could look forward to daily visits from her lover, smiling at his protestations that every hour spent away from her was like a lifetime. They dined together, walked in the gardens talking eagerly, and learned to know each other again as they renewed their vows of love.

Then he came to her one day, his face alight with joy.

'Mother and Letty have returned,' he said. 'Now, my dearest, we can decide upon our wedding day.' His mouth came down on hers in a passionate kiss.

'Would all your family care to dine here at the Mansion House?' she asked a little breathlessly.

'India and Isham hope that you will dine with them.

She plans to give a small party for you, your mother and father and your brother and sister, as well as Mair and Elspeth. Do say you agree! It would give her so much pleasure.'

'How can I refuse? She is so kind, and my parents will be delighted.'

It was no more than the truth. After their initial disappointment when they heard that her cousin was not to be her choice, George and Eliza Westcott had rejoiced in Gina's happiness.

'This is a surprise to us, my dear child, but I can't fault young Rushford,' her father had admitted. 'He's twice the man his father was, and his life has not been easy. It was pitiful to see all his efforts go for naught when Gareth Rushford was alive.'

'Now, Father, don't rake up old scandals,' Eliza Westcott begged. 'We've always liked Giles. He was such a merry lad and full of mischief, though there was no harm in him. I never found him other than polite. He'll make you happy, Gina, I am sure of it.'

They said as much to Giles, welcoming him as one of the family without the least trace of self-consciousness. George Westcott was his own man. He had done well in business and though he was aware of the social gulf between the aristocracy and those in trade, he sensed that times were changing. His wife was not so sure.

When Gina arrived with the invitation to dine with Lord and Lady Isham she met with some resistance from her mother.

'I don't know,' Eliza looked uncomfortable.

'We've been taught to keep our place, and to look up to our betters, not to dine with them.'

'Mother, please! How can you speak of "your betters"? Lord and Lady Isham are human beings like ourselves…no better and no worse… You knew India as a girl. How can you think that she has changed?'

'She's married to Lord Isham now…'

Gina laughed. 'So that is what is worrying you? Believe me, he is nothing like you might imagine. His boon companion at the moment is Mrs Clewes, the widow of a ship's chandler.'

This won a reluctant smile from Mrs Westcott. 'That may be so, but I can't abide that Rushford woman. She never exchanges a civil word with me.'

'I think you'll find she has changed.' Gina gave her mother a wicked look. 'Now I am her dearest Gina, a paragon of all the virtues…'

'Then she doesn't know you, love,' George Westcott chuckled. 'Come wife, your own daughter has a title now. You cannot let her down.'

It was enough to stifle all objections, and later that week, although claiming that she felt like Daniel about to enter the lion's den, Eliza Westcott accompanied her family to the Grange.

Her fears were soon allayed. Isham's easy greeting soon set his visitors at their ease, and Letty and India were their usual charming selves, insisting that Mrs Westcott sat between them.

'You shall not stand on ceremony, ma'am,' India said prettily. 'You've known us all our lives. May I

make you known to our dear Lucia, the Dowager
Lady Isham?'

Mrs Westcott nodded shyly.

'And here is Mrs Clewes, a friend of ours, as is Mr
Newby. My mother you know already as a neigh-
bour.'

'How pleased you must be to have dear Gina home
again,' Mrs Rushford gushed. 'And now to hear this
happy news! I declare that I am over the moon about
it...'

Eliza viewed the speaker with a sardonic eye. She
was under no illusions. Gina's fortune had brought
about this startling change in Mrs Rushford. Without
it the woman would not have given her the time of
day.

Mrs Rushford noticed nothing amiss. 'Two of my
children to be wed this year!' she continued in sentimental tones. 'I hope that you won't consider a double wedding, Gina? A bride's day should be hers
alone.'

'We haven't decided yet,' Gina said truthfully.

'Well, time enough, my dear. You will wish to go
to London for your bride-clothes. If you wish it I will
give you an introduction to Madame Félice... She has
provided Letty's trousseau.'

Gina laughed. 'I thank you, ma'am, but I think not.
I am not quite her style...'

'Perhaps not!' Mrs Rushford subjected her future
daughter-in-law to a searching inspection. 'Letty is,
after all, a beauty...not that you do not always look

charmingly, Gina, though you might consider something a little more modish.'

Gina hid a smile. Mrs Rushford's penchant for extravagant trimmings was well known. She could see no virtue in understated elegance. It had escaped her notice that Gina's shawl of the finest Norwich silk had cost the best part of fifty guineas.

'Well, Mama, at least you and Letty are prepared for all occasions.' India hastened to divert her mother's attention from Gina. She had caught her friend's eye and she realised that Gina was struggling to keep her countenance. 'I never saw so many packages in my life...'

'The shopping was tiring,' Mrs Rushford admitted grandly. 'You must blame Isham, my dear India. He insisted that Letty must have the best of everything.'

Letty shot an anxious glance at her brother-in-law. 'But not *quite* so much of everything,' she said in a low voice. 'Oh, Anthony, I am so sorry. I couldn't stop her. We shall be forever in your debt.'

Isham drew her into the window embrasure. 'Not nearly so much as I am in yours, Letty. Your mother was filling India's head with foolish fancies. Had you not taken her away I should have been forced to speak severely. That would have upset my darling wife.'

'India looks so much better now. Gina's company has been good for her, I think.'

'That's true! And now, with the two weddings to occupy your mother's mind, India will get some peace. When does Oliver arrive?'

'In time for the fête at Perceval Hall, I hope.' Letty

was radiant at the prospect of seeing her betrothed again. 'When I wrote I warned him of the date, so I expect him by Thursday at the latest. The fête is on the eighteenth, is it not?'

'It is. That is Friday of next week. I had best rally the troops. Lady Eleanor will be hoping for a good attendance…'

Mrs Rushford caught his last words. She leaned back in her chair with a gracious smile. 'My sister's gatherings are *always* well attended,' she announced. 'One is often surprised by some of the guests, but times are changing, as we all know, and the villagers enjoy the opportunity to mingle with their betters.' She leaned towards the Westcotts and for an awful moment India feared another gaffe. She was saved when dinner was announced.

Local gossip would prove to be the safest subject at the dinner table, she decided, but none of her guests could throw any further light upon the mysterious murder of the Marquis.

'But what of the Prince's men?' Gina was puzzled. 'Have they discovered nothing?'

'Not yet, so I understand.' Isham turned to Mr Westcott. 'What is your opinion, sir?'

'I won't speculate, my lord. The facts are few, it seems, in spite of the enquiries made throughout the village. Burneck, the single remaining servant at Steepwood Abbey, is thought to know far more than he'll admit. Pressure may be brought to bear on him… Otherwise he'll keep his secret.'

'Truth will out!' Mrs Clewes said cheerfully. 'I confess I'd like to know before I leave for Bristol…'

There was a general outcry.

'Ma'am, you don't think of leaving us yet?' India was dismayed. 'Won't you attend the fête?'

'I'd love to,' Mrs Clewes said promptly. 'But it's my feet, my dear. I ain't in the way of being able to walk about so much.'

'Then you shan't do so, my dear ma'am.' Isham grinned at her. 'If you'll accept the offer of a bath-chair I shall challenge you to a duel at the coconut shies…'

'Done! What is your wager, sir?'

'If you lose we hold you prisoner here for the rest of the summer…' He gave her a conspiratorial wink.

'Bless me, my lord, you'll have me ruined with this life of luxury.' Mrs Clewes beamed her pleasure at the invitation. 'I'll be naught but a parasite…'

'No, ma'am, I have ulterior motives. Giles tells me that you like a game of cards. With Mrs Rushford we shall make up a useful foursome…' Isham gave her a long look, and Mrs Clewes was quick to understand. With her support India would have some protection from her mother's gloomy prognostications.

'I play for pennies, sir, but there, you won't mind that. Besides, I don't intend to lose the wager…if this fine weather holds, which I make no doubt it will.'

She was right, and on the following Friday the entire party joined the queue of carriages at the entrance to Perceval Hall.

Mrs Rushford was in the best of humours. The long wait did not trouble her in the least as she nodded and smiled at her acquaintances.

'July is just the best of months for a function of this kind,' she said approvingly. 'With the Season over, so many of our friends are returned to the country. I declare, we shall never be at home. Since the announcement of your betrothal appeared in the London papers, Giles, we've had kind messages and invitations by every post.'

The villagers too were pressing close to the open carriage, offering their good wishes to the future bridegroom. India glanced at him and then at her sister.

'Dear Giles!' she said softly. 'He looks as radiant as any bride. Is it not wonderful?'

Letty pressed her hand, but her gaze was fixed on Oliver. 'We are all so lucky, India. A year ago we could not have imagined that we should be here, within weeks of our marriages to those we love so much.'

India looked at the sea of faces that surrounded her. 'Your weddings will be well attended, love. The news has spread like wildfire since the first of the banns was called.'

'I can't believe it yet,' Letty's eyes were dreamy. 'Oh, look! There is Gina with the girls...'

Giles was out of the carriage in an instant, though the procession was already beginning to move. Minutes later he handed Gina down, tucking her hand beneath his arm.

'Let me make you known to my aunt and uncle, my darling…' He glanced back to see his mother deep in conversation with one of her bosom bows.

Mrs Rushford had prepared her story carefully, stressing Gina's title, hinting at her fortune, and glossing over the previous background and unfortunate antecedents of her future daughter-in-law.

'Mother will be fully occupied for the day,' he predicted as they approached Sir James and Lady Perceval. 'Later we'll slip away somewhere on our own.'

Gina looked up at him with laughing eyes. 'And what of Mair and Elspeth?' she asked. 'I have certain responsibilities, my dear.'

'Nonsense!' he said fondly. 'Look at them! They have already found their friends…'

It was true. Mair and Elspeth were surrounded by a group of girls, many of whom attended Mrs Guarding's Academy, and included the Vicar's younger daughters, Frederica and Henrietta.

Gina was welcomed kindly by Sir James and Lady Perceval.

'Shall you care to attend the running races?' Lady Eleanor enquired. 'They are always well supported, and the Vicar will present the prizes…'

Gina and Giles strolled off in company with their host and hostess and for the next hour they were fully occupied in clapping home the various contestants. There was keen competition among the villagers for the chance to win a new smock for the men, and lengths of material and ribbons for the girls.

Giles looked round as the smell of roasting meat drifted across the lawns.

'I'm starving,' he announced 'Will the ox be ready, Aunt?'

'I hope so, Giles. The fire was lit at first light yesterday. Gina must be hungry too. Will you take her over to the tables?' She turned to Gina. 'In the ordinary way we should dine *en famille*, my dear, but today is open house, and all are welcome to as much as they can eat and drink. We don't stand on ceremony.'

Gina looked at the milling crowds. 'You are generous, ma'am.' She twinkled at her hostess. 'Your guests appear to be taking full advantage.'

'I'm glad of it,' her ladyship said simply. 'Times have been hard for everyone in these past years and we have felt so helpless. This is the least that we can do… Now off you go, and enjoy yourselves…'

'Your aunt feels strongly for the local people,' Gina observed as they strolled away. 'My mother and father have the highest praise for her.'

'She deserves it, Gina. Had Steepwood Abbey not have been lost to the Marquis, it would have been the Earl of Yardley who looked to the welfare of the villagers. Now those duties have fallen upon my aunts and both my uncles.'

'I'm glad that your uncle William is to marry us,' she told him shyly. 'Are you happy with this notion of a double wedding?'

For answer he slipped an arm about her waist and held her close. 'Can you doubt it? I'd have agreed to anything, my love, just so long as you become my bride.'

Gina blushed. 'People are looking at us, Giles.'

'Let them look!' He helped her to a generous portion of roast meat. 'I think we need not stay for long. No one will miss us in this crush if we slip away.'

'First I must find the girls and let them know. They will wonder if we are nowhere to be found.'

'Will they?' he teased. 'You forget, my darling, Mair and Elspeth are almost women grown, and Mair, in particular, soon found out our secret.'

'Even so, I don't wish to desert them.' Gina looked about her. 'I don't see them anywhere, do you?'

'Were they not with Frederica? She is with her sister, over there. Shall I ask for them?'

As he moved over to speak to the girls, Gina followed him.

'Why, Mr Rushford, we all went to see the hermit's grotto in the grounds,' Frederica told him. 'Mr Westcott sent us back to find some of our friends. He felt that they would like to see it…'

Gina's blood turned to ice in her veins. 'Mr Westcott? Are you speaking of my father?'

She knew the answer before the girls replied. 'No, ma'am,' Henrietta said politely. 'It was Mr Samuel Westcott who mentioned the grotto to us…'

'There now, you have no further need to worry…' Giles turned to Gina, only to find that her face was deathly pale.

'Where…where is this grotto?' she choked out.

'Why, ma'am, it is along that path…' The girls were startled by the urgency in Gina's voice.

'Giles, will you get my father?' Gina threw the words at him as she sped away. She was ploughing through mire on leaden feet, unable to gain speed. Pray heaven that she was not too late. Ignoring the stitch in her side, she hurried on, until the shell-lined grotto came into view.

Now common-sense returned. She slowed, approaching the grotto from the side. Hopefully, nothing untoward had happened. Peering into the gloom, all she could see was the vast bulk of her uncle. He seemed to be pleading with Elspeth.

'Were you hoping to see the hermit?' he asked. 'He won't appear if there are two of you.'

'I don't believe that there is a hermit,' Elspeth told him scornfully. 'How would he live here in the winter? This place is cold and damp.'

'Then fetch Gina,' he suggested. 'She will tell you the truth of it. Mair and I will wait for you…'

'I think not!' Gina stepped into the cavern. 'Mair, you and Elspeth must return to others…'

'But, Gina, this place is fascinating,' Elspeth stared at her. 'Just look at all the shells! It must have taken years to build them into the walls…'

'Do as I say!' Gina's voice was verging on hysteria. The girls did not argue further. They hurried away.

Samuel Westcott turned towards her, his small eyes alive with malice. 'Gina to the rescue?' he jeered. 'You'll do instead, my dear.'

Gina faced him squarely. 'I warned you, uncle,' she said quietly. 'This time you have gone too far…'

He laughed in her face. 'For showing the girls a grotto? It seems innocent enough to me…'

Gina stood her ground. 'I know you all too well,' she replied. 'You were trying to get rid of Elspeth. What would have happened had I not arrived?'

'Shall I show you, Gina?' He waddled towards her then, his fat hands reaching out for her. 'Are you to be wed? I'll have you first, you vixen.' Then he was upon her, tearing at her gown. 'I've waited long enough for this…'

Gina screamed as he ripped her bodice open to the waist. His hands were everywhere, fondling her breasts, sliding over her hips, and tugging at her skirts.

'Don't fight me!' he said thickly. 'You know it's what you want. How long is it since a man has bedded you?'

Gina didn't answer him. With a sigh she let herself grow limp within his grasp. To struggle would be useless. He was much too strong for her, but she might outwit him with guile.

'Fainted, have you?' he grunted. 'Pity! I wanted you to know exactly what I'm going to do to you…'

Gina thought quickly. Her thin kid slippers were too soft to hurt him if she kicked out, and he was holding her too close for her to raise a knee and sink it into that amorphous mass of flesh.

He shook her roughly, and when she didn't respond

he loosened his grip just enough for Gina to bend her arm. Then she drove her elbow into his stomach.

He doubled up with a gasp. He was standing between her and the narrow entrance to the grotto, but when she tried to push past him, his hand shot out and gripped her waist. Gina bent her head and tried to bite him, but he wound his fingers into her hair and pulled until the pain was unbearable.

'Still up to your old tricks, my girl? I've owed you something for these many years. Now It's time to pay…'

'Let me go!' she cried. 'Giles is following me…'

'Giles is following me!' he mimicked. 'He ain't here yet, my dear. Thought you'd trick me, didn't you, by making up to George? But I know you, you bitch! George ain't good enough for you. Will Rushford want my leavings…?'

Her situation was hopeless, but Gina fought him tooth and nail, clawing at his face and drawing blood.

With a curse he slapped her hard across the head, knocking her to the ground. Then he threw himself upon her, fumbling at her skirts.

Gina writhed beneath him, but she felt that she was suffocating. Nausea overcame her at the smell of his stale sweat, but the lascivious mouth came ever closer to her own.

Then, suddenly, the weight was gone and she heard a crash as her uncle was thrown bodily across the floor of the cave to land against the stone wall.

Giles was upon him in an instant, his hands around the bull neck. He hadn't uttered a word and somehow

his silence was more terrible than any shouts of out-
rage.

Gina watched in horror as Samuel Westcott's feet
began to drum upon the ground.

'No!' she cried. 'Don't kill him! He isn't worth a
hanging!'

Giles seemed not to have heard her as she struggled
painfully to her feet.

'Let him go, I beg of you!' Her hands were upon
her lover's shoulders, but he didn't look at her.

Then she was gently set aside, as her father took
her place. By exerting all his strength he broke the
death grip which Giles had upon his brother.

'Gina is right,' he said quietly. 'This animal isn't
worth a hanging. He won't trouble you again. I'll
make sure of that.' He looked in disgust at the cow-
ering man upon the ground.

'Get out!' he said in icy tones. 'You are no kin of
mine. Show your face in Abbot Quincey ever again
and I'll destroy you. Don't forget that I own most of
your London business…'

With a speed surprising in so large a man, Samuel
Westcott scuttled away.

Gina was shaking uncontrollably. Only the fact that
Giles was holding her enabled her to stand upright.

'Come out into the light,' he urged gently. 'Shall I
carry you, my love?'

'Just give me a moment,' she whispered. 'I shall
be perfectly all right.' Weakly, she tried to draw together the edges of her gown, which was ripped from

bodice to hemline. 'It's ruined!' she said inconsequentially. Then she burst into tears.

'My dear child!' Her father was still deeply shocked. 'Let me take you home... You need to rest...'

'Sir, with respect, I will take Gina home. If you'd be good enough to find the girls and follow us...?'

'No!' Gina wiped away her tears. 'No one must ever know what has happened here. Let the girls stay... I want to change before I see them.'

'Then I'll come with you to the Mansion House,' her father said firmly. 'I have much to say to you...' His eyes were so sad that Gina reached out to him.

'How much did you hear?' she asked.

'Enough to know the answers to much that has puzzled me for years. Why did you not tell me, Gina?'

'I couldn't!' she confessed. 'He is your own brother. Would you have believed me?'

'I no longer have a brother,' he said sternly. 'Was this why you ran away from us, my dear?'

She nodded, but she could not trust herself to give him the details of those far-off attempts upon her virtue.

'I've been a fool,' George Westcott said. 'The truth has been staring me in the face for years. Other incidents have been reported to me. I didn't believe any of the complaints, putting them down to envy and ill-will.'

'It's over now,' she comforted. 'You know the truth about him. He will not face you ever again.'

Gina turned to Giles. 'Will you take me home, my darling?'

Wordlessly, he put his arm about her and held her close, burying his face in her hair.

'I might have been too late,' he whispered. 'When you were most in need of me I wasn't there... Oh, my dear, why did you decide to confront your uncle on your own?'

'I didn't think,' she told him frankly. 'When I heard that he was alone with Mair and Elspeth I forgot the danger. I'd fought him off before, you know.'

Giles held her away from him and looked down at the vivid little face.

'What am I to do with you, my love? Will you still be ·battling on when we are old and grey, forgetting that you have a husband to take care of you?'

'I doubt that I shall forget my husband...' Gina raised her face to his, reaching up to trace the outlines of his mobile mouth with her fingertips. 'You are dearer to me than life itself...'

He kissed her then, and the world was lost to them as they pledged their love in a passionate embrace.

Gina released herself at last, and, blushing, she looked round for her father. Discreetly, George Westcott had disappeared.

'We had best go before we are discovered.' Gina managed a faint smile. 'I am in no fit state to greet the world at present.'

Giles grinned at her. 'Fear not! Our friends will think only that my passion got the better of me...'

'Why, Giles, that would cause a scandal!'

'And shall you care, my love? What happened to the woman who had no regard for conventions?'

'I intend to change when we are married,' she said demurely.

'God forbid!' Giles looked at her in mock horror. 'What shall I do for entertainment…?'

'I'm sure you'll think of something…' With a wicked smile Gina whisked away from him and slipped through the entrance to the grotto.

As Gina had hoped, no breath of scandal was ever attached to the sudden departure of Samuel Westcott from Abbot Quincey. He'd given pressure of business as his excuse, and this was generally accepted. George gave a sigh of relief and announced his intention to marry Ellie without delay, since Gina was already spoken for and his father could no longer pressure him.

Gina herself had soon recovered from her ordeal. As her wedding day approached she was fully occupied in making arrangements for Mair and Elspeth to stay with India for the duration of her honeymoon.

'Are you quite sure?' she asked anxiously. 'The girls would be happy to visit their relations in Scotland.'

'Oh, let us have them,' India begged. 'It is such fun to have the young about the place…'

'But you say that about the old, my dear. What of Mrs Clewes?'

'Gina, she is a boon! My mother is now fully occupied. Mrs Clewes is a marvel. Mama has not even interfered in the arrangements for your wedding…'

'Still playing cards?' Gina twinkled at her friend.

'That, and gossip, my dear. Anthony is off on some mysterious errand at this very moment. He won't get through the doorway before they pounce on him…'

There was much truth in her remarks, but Lord Isham was looking thoughtful as he entered the room.

'Anthony, what is it?' India's eyes searched her husband's face. 'Do you bring us news?'

'I do.' Isham sat down by her and took her hand. 'I'm sure it will delight you. I hear that there is now a real possibility that the Earl of Yardley will regain possession of the Abbey.'

There was a general murmur of approval.

'Is it certain?' Giles said doubtfully. 'I thought there was at present no visible owner…'

'It won't happen overnight,' Isham agreed. 'But, as you know, Yardley was in the process of negotiating to buy it back from Sywell, though the sale was not confirmed before the Marquis died.'

'But what of the Marchioness? Suppose she reappears?' India looked concerned.

'Yardley has considered that possibility. If his lands are returned to him and she returns he has promised that she will be cared for, both financially and in every other way.'

'How like him!' India's face was alight with pleasure. 'Oh, my dear, just think what it will mean to the local people to have Yardley back again! How soon shall we be certain?'

'Not before November, I imagine. There are the legalities to consider, and these matters take time. Representations have been made to the authorities.'

Isham saw that Mrs Clewes was looking puzzled. 'Ma'am?'

'I was just wondering, My Lord…who is the Earl of Yardley? I have not heard of him…'

Mrs Rushford gave a gusty sigh. 'My dear Madam, the Earls of Yardley were the greatest landowners in this district. They have owned Steepwood Abbey for generations, that is, until some twenty years ago, when the place was gambled away to Sywell.'

'All of it?' Thomas Newby was incredulous. 'The Earl could not have been in his right mind…'

'He wasn't!' Giles said bluntly. 'Mother, you know the story better than any of us. Won't you explain?'

Delighted to be the centre of attention, Isabel Rushford settled back in her chair. 'It started with a scandal,' she said with relish. 'Viscount Angmering, Yardley's eldest son, returned from his Grand Tour with some young French aristocrat. The Earl refused his consent to the marriage because the girl was a Catholic. When Angmering refused to give her up his father threw him off.'

Mrs Clewes pursed her lips in disapproval. 'I'd have stood by my child no matter what he'd done,' she announced.

'And so would I!' India said warmly. 'Up to and including murder!'

'Women!' Isham shook his head at them but he was smiling. 'Isabel, will you go on?'

'Well, the news came from France that Angmering had been killed in a bread riot. His father was distraught, blaming himself for banishing his heir. The Earl went up to town and started drinking. Somehow he found himself in Sywell's company at one of the gambling clubs. That night he lost everything at the tables—the Abbey, his lands, the house in town and his estates in the north of England. Then he shot himself...'

India looked at her mother in concern. Mrs Rushford was pale and trembling. Her story was all too close to home. To a lesser extent Gareth Rushford had done the same.

Isham offered her a glass of wine, but she waved it away, determined to continue her story. 'Thomas Cleeve is the present Earl. He inherited after the death of the Earl and Viscount Angmering. He's tried for years to buy back Steepwood Abbey.'

'He's wealthy, then?' Mrs Clewes was fascinated.

'He made his fortune in India, so I understand. I never heard scandal of him. What a boon it would be to have the family back at Steepwood Abbey...'

'Most certainly.' Isham looked round at the assembled company. 'Yardley takes his responsibilities seriously. Already he has paid off monies owed to the local tradesmen, but we must be patient. Now it has been discovered that Sywell gained the Abbey by murdering the old Earl, rather than honourably, if all goes well the present Earl's heritage will be restored to him before the year's end.'

'And then?' Giles questioned.

'Why, then the local people may look forward to better times. There will be work for all. Yardley intends to restore the Abbey and improve his lands. He speaks of repairing the workers' cottages, hedging, ditching, rotation of crops, and general profitability.'

Giles did not attempt to hide his pleasure. 'And the tenant farmers on his land? Are they to get some help?'

'With your assistance, Giles. The Earl is hoping to see you soon. He intends to make full use of your inventions.'

'Then we must invite him to our wedding.' Gina's smile was radiant. 'Will he come, do you suppose?'

'I don't doubt it, Gina.'

Isabel Rushford touched a handkerchief to her eyes. 'Just two more days and my children will be gone from me,' she mourned. 'What it is to be old and lonely…!'

'You will be much in need of company,' Isham agreed. 'What do you say to a trip to Brighton with Mrs Clewes? Many of your bosom bows will be there for the Prince's stay. He will be happy to make your acquaintance…'

Mrs Rushford brightened at once. 'Do you say that we shall be received at the Pavillion by the Prince himself? That is something I have dreamed of. We shall meet the highest in the land…and the shops…! Oh, my dears, if my health will stand it, I shall be happy to undertake the journey.' Then she bethought herself of her proposed companion. 'Mrs Clewes may not wish to go…' she said sadly.

'Whyever not?' the lady replied. Earlier she had been primed by Isham, who assured her that the Prince was anxious to make her acquaintance. Isham was on safe ground. He had already entertained the Prince with stories of the redoubtable widow from Bristol, and he knew that Mrs Clewes was quite in the Regent's style.

'Then if you insist...!' Mrs Rushford allowed herself to be persuaded into undertaking an extravagant holiday at her son-in-law's expense.

'This is such a happy time for all of us,' she said brightly.

That sentiment was echoed in many a heart.

On the day of the wedding the sun shone upon both brides. They arrived together at the church in Abbot Quincey, with Letty upon Isham's arm and Gina with her father.

The crowds overflowed into the churchyard, commenting with awed approval upon the gowns, the bonnets, the flowers, and the handsome appearance of the guests.

Gina was unaware of it. She had dressed with care that morning in an elegant gown of finest ivory silk beneath a tunic of spider lace in the same shade. A tiny head-dress sat upon her shining hair, trimmed only with a few pearls.

She would never outshine the beautiful Letty, and she had no intention of doing so. The girl beside her was a vision of loveliness in her bridal gown, but the onlookers could not decide which of the two looked the happier.

For Gina there was only Giles, waiting for her at the altar steps. She looked long into his eyes, and saw there a man restored to love and life, waiting to claim her as his bride.

When they made their vows she found that she was trembling, but he gave her hand a reassuring squeeze, and she smiled up at him with misty eyes.

The rest of the day had a dreamlike quality and later she had little recollection of the celebrations, the sumptuous wedding breakfast at Perceval Hall, and the congratulations of her friends.

Giles stole her away at last, laughing as he hurried her to the waiting carriage.

'I thought we'd never get away,' he said, as he slipped his arm about her waist. 'Now I can kiss you as I've longed to do all day, my darling wife.'

Gina lifted her face to his. 'Is it really true?' she asked in wonder. 'I can't believe that we are wed at last.'

'Why, Mrs Rushford, I am deeply shocked! Here we are, about to live together for the next fifty years or so, and you doubt that we are wed?'

Gina hid her face in his coat. She was blushing deeply. 'Don't tease!' she whispered. 'Giles, I have not told you this before, but I have never been a wife in the true sense.'

He looked down at her and his eyes were filled with tenderness. 'I guessed as much, my dear one. You have never lost that look of innocence you had when I first met you.'

'Then I did not deceive you?'

'Never, Gina!' His lips found hers in a lingering kiss, and Gina forgot the wasted years in an over-whelming sense of rapture. She threw her arms about his neck, murmuring inarticulate words.

His heart beat strongly against her own and she revelled in the old familiar sensation of his closeness, his strength, and the delicious feeling of being pro-tected from all harm.

'I love you so,' she whispered.

'Then show me!' he demanded as he nibbled gently at her ear.

Gina threw all decorum to the winds as she cupped his face within her hands and drew it down to hers. She teased him then with feather-light caresses, trac-ing the curve of his eyebrows with her fingertips, dropping kisses upon his eyelids, and finally seeking his mouth.

The strength of his response left her breathless, but she looked at him with perfect trust. 'I want you, my love,' she said. 'When you make me your wife in truth, my happiness will be complete.'

Giles kissed her again, and in that kiss there was the promise of a lifetime of devotion.

* * * * *

Modern Romance™
...seduction and
passion guaranteed

Tender Romance™
...love affairs that
last a lifetime

Sensual Romance™
...sassy, sexy and
seductive

Blaze
...sultry days and
steamy nights

Medical Romance™
...medical drama on
the pulse

Historical Romance™
...rich, vivid and
passionate

29 new titles every month.

*With all kinds of Romance for
every kind of mood...*

MILLS & BOON®

Makes any time special™

MAT4

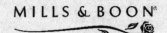
0402/AWARD

0702/73/MB38

Coming in July

❧

The Ultimate Betty Neels Collection

❧

✳ A stunning 12 book collection beautifully packaged for you to collect each month from bestselling author Betty Neels.

✳ Loved by millions of women around the world, this collection of heartwarming stories will be a joy to treasure forever.

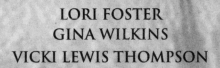